Intercession

Nyneve Ransom

I0673764

Saturnian Press

Printed in the United States of America.

First Printing, 2016

ISBN 978-0-9972379-7-9 (Paperback)
ISBN 978-0-9972379-8-6 (Kindle)
ISBN 978-0-9972379-9-3 (EPUB)

Saturnian Press
4207 SE Woodstock Blvd #420
Portland, OR 97206
saturnianpress.com

Layout: LibreOffice
Fonts: Garamond No 8, League Gothic

For Tova.
May you live forever.

Thanks to:

    NaNoWriMo, for the challenge.

    Jay, for hours at the coffee shop.

    Kirsten, for everything.

    Claudia, for the countless edits.

    John, Dustin, Jen, and Adam, for the suggestions.

Intercession

2014, September 30th, Tuesday

The bullet passed through Rob's shoulder and the familiar pain knocked any useful thoughts from his mind. He slumped against the brick wall, landing in a pile of full trash bags that had never made their way into the neighboring garbage cart. The ground in the parking lot was wet from the recent drizzle. Rob's assailant lowered his gun and started swearing to himself, "Shit. Why couldn't you just hand over the cash?"

"Owww, dammit," was initially all Rob could offer in reply. His eyes focused again in the early evening light as he felt hands searching through his jacket pockets. His shoulder finished healing.

Rob grabbed the mugger's wrist and yanked down, watching his eyes go wide. As the gun came up again, level with Rob's head, he deflected it hard, leaving his attacker's arm swung wide. Off balance, leaning over Rob, the mugger got a forehead to his nose as Rob stood up with purpose.

As the mugger fell backwards, the gun flew from his hand and bounced off the wall, clattering across the slick pavement. Rob retrieved it as the mugger tried to sit up, holding his bleeding face with both hands.

Rob turned back around to face the mugger, with the tables turned. Instead of aiming, he walked directly up to the mugger and pressed the muzzle against his cheek.

"Wai—wait! Don't kill me!" stammered the mugger.

"Why? You just tried to kill me over twenty dollars. How many people have you robbed walking out of that 7-11? I just wanted to go see a movie, and now I'm going to have to kill you, which is really going to change the tenor of my night," Rob muttered, almost to himself.

"No, wait, it was a joke! You look fine! I was just trying to scare you! Please man, no harm done, my face is okay, I'll just go away, you see that movie, I've got kids I gotta feed!" the mugger pleaded.

"I wish I could claim self-defense," Rob hissed at the man. "But I don't feel much like trying to stuff your body in the ground. I know your face. This is my city, and if I ever see you again, it'll be your last."

"Thank—"

Rob shifted his weight slightly, bringing the muzzle away from the mugger's face, and fired into the bricks. The mugger ducked down and away, shrieking while Rob continued to fire, chips of the wall spraying both of them. The gun clicked one final time, the magazine empty. Rob stared at the terrified mugger, who was holding his ear and screaming. Both the mugger's face and Rob's hand bled from brick fragments.

"Don't forget," Rob reminded.

The mugger just stared, anger starting to build behind his eyes.

"I'll keep this," Rob lied as he stuffed the pistol into his jacket. He idly wiped the blood off his hand before asking, "Give me your cell phone."

"You must be craz—"

"NOW!"

The mugger fished around in his pocket and produced a small flip-phone, handing it up to Rob. Rob snatched it from the mugger's quavering grip and dialed 911, "Hello? Yes, I'd like to report what sounded like gun fire. I think someone's been shot in the 7-11 parking lot at 97th and Foster."

The mugger slipped as he struggled to get up. Finding his feet, and still holding his ear, he started to run. The 7-11 cashier came around the corner of the building just as the mugger dashed past.

Rob turned away, snapped the phone in half and dropped it. He continued his walk north up Foster. The cashier wouldn't have seen his face, and he was going to need a new jacket anyway. It was still early; daylight savings hadn't kicked in yet. The 9 p.m. show time Rob wanted to make wasn't for another couple hours so he still had time to walk home and change shirts. He'd never been attacked on any of his day-long walks through Portland before. That was a new experience!

Rob picked brick fragments out of his jacket as cop cars shot past heading south, sirens blaring. He crouched down at the edge of the sidewalk and pitched the pistol into a sewer drain. Painted on the street just below the sewer was a picture of a salmon, with the text "Protect the Columbia River. Only rain down the drain." Rob smiled to himself and wondered if some city worker was going to be seriously surprised by a free gun. Or not … if the rain kept up, the sewers would overflow into the river, just like the sign warned. Maybe the salmon could put a gun to good use in reestablishing their upriver homes.

Rob moved his recently acquired, trouble-causing $20 from his jacket pocket to the front pocket of his jeans, and pulled off his jacket. He inspected the bullet hole. Like in most ballistic tests, it had made a small puncture in the front, and a larger spread of shredded material on the back. His T-shirt was similar, though it had blood visible on the front. Rob figured the back was even worse looking. He poked his shoulder idly. Not even a scratch. Walking down the street with either the jacket on, the shirt on, or shirtless was going to call attention to him, so he threw the jacket over his back and tied its arms around his neck like he was from the 80s. The sleeves covered the blood well enough. He'd probably blend in with the hipsters on the way to the Pearl District long enough to make it home, wash up, and get changed.

After an hour of walking up Foster, across the Ross Island Bridge, along the river front, and up into the Pearl, he let himself into his condo. He ditched his shirt and jacket into the garbage, and took a quick shower to wash off the mud, blood, and bits of bone and brick.

He'd been fond of the jacket, even if the left pocket's zipper had started sticking. It had served him pretty well the past 20 years or so, and he was pissed he'd have to find a replacement. There was a Columbia store nearby and that was probably where he got the last one.

He plucked a fresh T-shirt out of his dresser and went to find a temporary jacket replacement. The maids from the service kept his condo in pristine condition, though they rearranged his closets too frequently. It was usually for the better, and he was able to find what he wanted, but he just kind of wished things could just stay the same from year to year. It was a constant reminder of his condition.

One place the maids didn't touch was his office. His current journal was locked in his desk drawer, with the last few years' worth in the fire safe he'd installed at the back of the room. For journals prior to that, he had his collection in a concrete bunker in the Cascade Mountains.

He flipped through the journal and started a new entry. He made some quick observations about his walk on the east side of the city and then detailed what had happened with the mugger. It was hardly the worst thing that had ever happened to him, but he knew he'd want to remember it later so he wrote it all down. He hadn't gotten very far with his indexing project, and he kept swearing he'd switch to digital, but it seemed like such a giant task. With so much to transcribe, he kept hoping he could just wait it out until OCR was good enough with cursive, or at least speech-to-text could keep up with narration. When that happened, he could do some kind of reverse audio-book where he'd just read journals out loud while he walked and it'd be converted into text. From there he'd have an easier time with indexing people and events.

Right now the only thing he'd switched to doing digitally was managing his holdings. That had gotten pretty complex even by the 50s, but now it was relatively easy to keep track of each of his shell companies, their investments, the hoards of lawyers responsible for each entity, and the various countries of origin.

He gazed out his 10th floor window and lingered on the view across downtown Portland's glowing night lights. The journal entry was complete and he still had enough time to call a cab to Cinema 21. Rob walked back through the condo and glanced at his television. He preferred watching most things from the privacy of his own home, but going to the theater brought him back in time a little. He still missed Marie. She'd loved movies as much as he did. It had been so long now, but he could still remember her face beaming up at the screen at the Grand Café in Paris. It was a captivating experience and they were hooked.

It was fading, but he remembered the end, too. He tried to push it from his mind but it always popped up when he wanted it least. They'd spent almost 30 years together, mostly in London. When the first World War came, Rob, then known as Leland, had enlisted to fight the Germans. Marie had supported the decision. Neither of them wanted to be apart but they both knew he'd be safe. Rob always wanted to help make things right, but normally there was no way to be subtle. However, war was not remotely subtle, so he figured he'd be quite successful there. The trick was avoiding notoriety.

He had journals filled with the stuff. It was all a blur now. Trenches, bayonets, grenades. The grenades worked best. Regardless, the real pain was on the return from his tour in early 1919. Like so many others, Marie had caught the Spanish Flu. There was nothing to stop it and, just before May, she had died. Rob had lost many friends to the war, to the flu, and to time, but Marie had been the first and the last person to know him for what he truly was. He'd never been able to fully share it with anyone else. A few people had suspected, but most found ways to convince themselves that it was just a mistake, a trick of the light, or a misunderstanding. His friends all just thought he had a hardy constitution. And, excepting his life with Marie, he was never in one place long enough for people to notice that he wasn't aging.

2014, October 1ˢᵗ, Wednesday

Hani slowly closed the lid of her laptop. She was close to finding Reese, and all that was left was a visit to some new friends in Salem. She was sure he was here in Oregon but there wasn't a good way to get access to the DMV's photo records. None of the nation-wide ID legislation had gotten anywhere, so her access to Federal records hadn't been much help to her.

Her vacation time from Oklahoma was starting to run thin. She'd saved up enough to spend a chunk of time in Eugene, Oregon. This was the last location where Reese had drawn a Social Security check. No one she'd talked to at the agency really considered it worth their time to investigate. They mostly wanted to go after larger scale fraud: stolen identities, family members collecting Social Security money for decades after someone had died, and the like. They rolled their collective eyes at her when she tried to get help to track down Reese's case.

He'd gone missing while traveling across the country, leaving a trail of cashed checks which came to a dead stop in Eugene. The last two checks were cashed at the same downtown bank. The six months prior were scattered across the country, leading slowly west. No one at the agency cared since, if it was fraud, it had stopped. And more importantly, it had stopped almost 20 years ago. The real issue was that Hani couldn't get into the specifics of her interest in this situation since no one would believe her.

She took a sip of her coffee, and set it back down. She picked up the copy of the photo she'd found in the Eugene Register-Guard newspaper archives. It had been taken during the 1997 Celebration Parade and Reese was plainly visible at the front of the spectators on the sidewalk. She'd almost lost hope flipping through years of the archived photos. She'd started looking through the collection from 1995. Reese had cashed a check in May and then June of that year, and she was certain he had stayed there longer.

When she'd first started looking for him, she struck out in every state she checked on. There was no Carl Reese on record with any DMV. There'd been absolutely no photo record of him that she could find. Federal records were very thin, and the biggest footprint he'd made had been retiring and drawing Social Security checks. She only knew what he looked like because he'd visited her office in early 1995.

Every few years, she'd spend another dollop of time trying to find more details but this was by far the biggest step she'd made. She carefully put the photo back in its sleeve and started packing up her things. She drained her coffee and looked around the Starbucks for the recycling. Or the composting. She couldn't really tell which she was supposed to use. She pitched the cardboard cup into the recycling and walked back to her rental car.

The drive to Salem was uneventful. It was raining lightly and Interstate 5 was mostly clear. A little over an hour later, she pulled in to the Oregon Department of Motor Vehicles Headquarters parking lot. She walked briskly through the maze of cars and in the front doors. She stopped at the information desk and got directions to Janet Krause's office.

Letting herself through the second floor office door, she smiled, "Hello! I'm here to see Ms Krause. I'm Hanielle Gittel."

The receptionist looked up and smiled back, "Hi, sure. I'll tell her you're here." He picked up the phone, pressed a single number, paused, and said "Hi, Ms Gittel is here to see you ... Sure, thanks." He set the phone down and gestured to the hall on his left, "She's at the end on the right."

"Thanks," Hani said and made her way down the hall. She tried to gather her nerve and suppress her excitement. "Hello," she said, after rounding the office door, "I'm Hani."

Janet looked up, "Hello, please sit down. How can I help you?"

Hani took a seat and pulled the photo from her bag. "I'm trying to locate someone who I think is responsible for identity theft and possibly Social Security fraud. He's been especially tricky to track down, but I finally got a workable photo of his face. As I understand it, you're heading up the facial recognition project here at the DMV. I was hoping you could take it for a spin and help me find this guy."

Janet grinned, "Well, I can do my best. You said on the phone you're with the Social Security Administration?"

"Yeah, been working there for about 20 years now," Hani replied. She fished her employee ID badge out of her bag and set it on Janet's desk.

"Watch out, you'll turn into a lifer like me!" Janet quipped, taking a quick glance at the ID. "Whatcha got?"

Hani handed the photo over to Janet. "Here's the only photo I've been able to find." She hadn't meant to say "I." She needed to continue to make this feel like an official investigation. "Our office security cameras were destroyed so this is all we have for him. No other states have DMV records under this name, and Eugene was the last place he left a trail."

Janet opened the folder and studied the photo, "Wow, when was this taken? That's some serious fashion time-travel."

"This is from 1997."

"Okay. It's straight-on, no hat, no facial hair ... I should be able to blow it up without much problem." She placed the photo face-down on the scanner next to her keyboard and started mousing around her screen, clicking purposefully.

"Thanks for taking the time to help us," Hani said, relaxing into her chair a bit.

"Sure thing. Okay, I've got it parameterized ... I'm putting it through the search system now. Shouldn't take much time at all," Janet said, leaning back, eyes glued to the screen. "Okay, I've got six high-confidence hits. This one looks the most like your photo, with the age-projection taken into account," Janet turned her screen towards Hani, who was already out of her seat and stretching across the desk to get a better view.

"It does, but this one here is him, I'm sure of it," Hani pointed to the fifth match.

Janet clicked through, and read back details, "That's from his 2005 renewal photo. I've got an address in Portland, and it looks like he goes by 'Robert McBride' now." Janet clicked some more and her printer hummed to life. "Here's a copy."

Hani stared at the DMV record. This was him. He didn't look a day older. First licensed in Oregon in May of 1995, one month before "Reese" vanished. "This is terrific. This is the first real break we've had on this investigation. The rest of my office was getting tired of me trying to find him."

Janet smiled, "Great! This is the reason I've been pushing for this project. Please keep me posted on the progress you make with the investigation. I'd love to include some details when I report on our successes here."

"Absolutely. It looks like my next stop is the FBI in Portland.

We'll have to work to tie McBride to Reese before I can do much more, but this is where it starts. Thank you so much for your time!"

Janet scooped the photo up from her scanner and handed it back to Hani, who fumbled a bit getting the DMV record and photo back into the folder. Hani stuffed the folder into her bag and said her goodbyes before winding her way out of the building. She only had tomorrow and Friday left on her vacation. She'd have to push her return flight to Oklahoma to Sunday night ... she had no idea what she was going to need to do next. The only thing she knew for sure was that she was *not* headed to the FBI office. She needed to confront Reese ... McBride ... directly and privately.

Back in her car, she stowed her bag safely on the passenger seat and pulled out her phone to browse through hotel options near McBride's address on NW 13th. Nothing nearby was cheap, so she backed off to something less expensive and further out. If parking was expensive on the street, she'd just hoof it from the hotel to start her stalking. A few clicks, typing of her credit card details, and she was set up.

With accommodations handled, she studied his address again. Zooming in on the map, she noticed the location wasn't an apartment but rather a commercial mail receiver. This wasn't his home—this was where his mail got delivered. Groaning, pondering her short time, she put away her phone and started the car. She still needed to get to Portland, even if she wasn't going to be able to just knock on his door.

She drove out through Salem, and headed back to I5, continuing north to Portland. She swiped at her phone and declared, "Dial office."

"Dialing office," her phone echoed.

After a few moments the line rang briefly and got picked up, "Hello, Social Security."

"Hi Dale, this is Hani calling."

"Oh hey Hani, I thought you were on vacation?"

"I am, but I got a hit on some possible identity theft in Oregon," Hani admitted.

"Oh no, not this again. Still trying to get yourself fired?" Dale ribbed.

"Ha ha," Hani droned sarcastically. "No, this might be something current. Can you do a quick check on an employment history for me?"

"Yeah, sure. Shoot."

Hani read back the details on Robert McBride's DMV record while trying to keep an eye on the road.

Some abbreviated tapping could be heard on Dale's side of the conversation as he poked the information into his computer. "Looks like he's been working in Oregon his whole life. First retirement payment was in 93. All to one address in Eugene, until he moved to Portland in 1999."

Hani frowned. Could this guy really have set himself up before driving out west? "Is the address the same as what I gave you?"

"Yeah, been there the whole time," Dale said.

"Okay, thanks. I'll keep you posted. This might be a false alarm," Hani lied.

"You bet. See you Monday," Dale said before he hung up.

Hani stared at the slowly approaching horizon.

1995, April 19th

He hated the snags in his well-planned transition to the West Coast, and he really didn't want to just scrap the plan he'd worked so hard on. He'd ruled out carrying a giant bag of cash for his year of cross-country travel, so he had been having his monthly retirement checks sent to his various stop-overs. However, the paperwork for his change of address for his layover in Oklahoma hadn't gone through. As a result, he'd needed to get someone to manually forward the last two months' worth of checks from Chicago to Oklahoma. He was still practicing being Carl Reese, so the delay wasn't a total loss.

He'd mostly started to convincingly respond to people calling him "Mr Reese" even though it'd only been a few months into using the "travel across the country on a retirement trip" cover. These maneuvers were always such a pain to get right, but he really couldn't stay in one place for more than a couple decades. He still had a way to go before he'd have reasonable access to the money he'd been shifting around. For now, he'd have to stay away from it and use the Social Security payouts from his employment history for Carl Reese's entire "life." It was technically legitimate: "Carl" hadn't worked a day in his life, but he'd filed solid W2s since the 1950s, and the United States had gladly accepted his income tax and Social Security payments the whole time.

This business with the address change, though, was annoying. He'd had to wait for the forwarded checks in Oklahoma, and that had forced a delay in his time-line. To be on schedule again for his transition plan in Eugene, he'd just have to skip Las Vegas. There wasn't time for that detour if he was going to thoroughly explore Yellowstone first. He didn't want the mail for his Eugene address change paperwork to drift its way through the system, possibly getting lost again. Since there was a Social Security office nearby in Oklahoma City, he decided to just head there instead to handle it in person. This was a bit of a risk since he didn't look like he was 65 years old, but he really didn't want to miss Yellowstone.

It was still pretty early in the morning, but they'd opened at 8, so he finished breakfast, collected his Reese papers, and drove downtown. The sky was clear, and Carl tried to avoid day-dreaming about his Yellowstone trip. He'd never been there before and it sounded amazing. He wanted to see if he could find some bears; he'd only ever seen them pacing around in cages in the Franklin Park Zoo and that was depressing. He wanted to see them in their real life.

He was not succeeding in his anti-daydream endeavor so he tried focusing harder on the road. He really didn't need to get pulled over and leave a blip of information behind from having his Massachusetts Driver's License run. That put his previous life unnecessarily close to this life. Intentionally, "Carl Reese" had no Driver's License at all, which seemed like a good way to separate the past from his donning the Robert McBride life in Portland in a few years.

He parked and made his way into the building. He paused at the metal detector and dropped his keys into a little bin for the X-Ray machine. He nodded to the guard who politely nodded back while waving him through and glancing up at the metal detector lights. Luckily, Carl's secrets were not ferrous.

There was no line at the Social Security Administration's door so he let himself in. There was one position staffed at the counter.

The woman behind the counter looked up and waved him over. The name plate next to her said "Hanielle Gittel." She smiled and greeted him, "Hi, how can I help you?"

"Hi Ms Gittel. I've got a little problem with my address on file," Carl started to explain. "I'd sent in a change of address, but I think it got lost. This is the old address and the new address, and here's my Social Security card."

"Okay, sure. I can help with that. Do you have any photo ID? I just need to—"

Suddenly Carl couldn't hear anything and the world flashed red and white. The woman in front of him seemed to flicker like a movie projector skipping a few frames. He registered pain almost everywhere and realized he and the room were on fire. His left arm was missing, along with a good chunk of his abdomen. He felt his left hip already resetting itself, binding muscle and bone back together, while his guts refilled and his skin snapped back across his side. His ribs stretched around his new organs again and, through the outstanding agony and numbness, he felt his left arm manifesting itself. He stumbled back, recoiling against the shock wave that had just passed through the building. The floor behind him had been torn up and tossed across the room, through him, across the counter, and into the back offices. Blinking, he refocused on the woman standing on the other side of the counter, impossibly unharmed. She was holding her ears, staring wide-eyed at him. Then the blazing ceiling collapsed and crushed him to the floor, along with everything else in the room.

* * *

Hani looked up from her game of solitaire as a well-dressed man somewhere in his 30s came through the door to her office. She waved him over and started working. The name on his Social Security card said Carl Reese. She was in the middle of asking for more ID when the room exploded. She felt herself skipping again. The world took on the familiar stuttering. One moment Carl was standing in front of her, and the next he looked like he'd been cut in half. His arm was missing and blood was pouring out over his belt from a cavernous mess where the left side of his torso used to be. Flames seemed to appear out of nowhere and she couldn't hear anything but maybe her own shriek of surprise.

Carl staggered slightly as he suddenly stopped bleeding like someone had turned off a faucet. The place where he used to have an arm throbbed and inflated. His left arm snapped into place like it'd never been missing. Hani stared in shock and confusion before the room's ceiling fell through her. She was, once again, absent from reality. Everything went quiet and her vision switched to high-speed. She felt herself drifting up and to the right. The flames only lasted an instant. After that, she could only see concrete, wood splinters and papers flashing by, then a bright flare of blue sky and she felt herself sag back into the real world.

"I found one! She's alive!" a voice shouted from somewhere behind her. It looked like it was late afternoon now. She wasn't sure if it had been more than a day or not but, by the looks of the heavy equipment around her, the rescue workers had been clearing debris and looking for bodies for some time. She was standing, just as she'd been when the room collapsed. She lowered her hands from her ears as a large man in an orange vest and a yellow hard hat stepped around in front of her, "Ma'am, are you okay? Are you hurt? Let me help you out of here."

"No, I'm ... I'm okay. I just managed to climb free just now,"

Hani tried to cover. The rescue workers didn't need much convincing, she was scratched up pretty well, and filthy, but nothing life-threatening ... as always. "What happened?"

"We're still not sure, but it seems someone blew up a truck. Some kind of terrorist attack," the man said, escorting her across bent rebar and chunks of concrete.

"Are ... is—" Hani stopped short. "How many people died?"

"I don't know for sure Ma'am. Let's get you patched up first," he said as medics rushed over to meet them at the edge of what used to be the building foundation.

Several weeks after the bombing at the Oklahoma City Federal Building, Hani had gotten most of the details she'd wanted. The two other coworkers of hers in the office that day had died in the collapse. They were lightly staffed that day, and it was still early. Her two friends, and the other 166 people who died, hadn't had the benefit of her strange affliction. They'd also found an "unmatched arm" which was burned too badly for fingerprinting.

Hani tried to suggest that it was Carl Reese's arm, but no one by that name was ever admitted to the hospital and no one matching his description was recorded at the scene. By the time the FBI checked up on him, he was cashing his Social Security checks in Oregon. They did note that they couldn't find a phone number or a home address for him, but ultimately they weren't interested since they had more important things to be doing. Hers was just one of almost 28,000 interviews they performed while constructing their case against McVeigh. They told her that he seemed to have nothing to do with the bombing and if she thought he was fraudulently drawing Social Security it should be investigated through her office instead.

She'd come up with nothing on her end either. The Federal

Building's security cameras and their recordings were destroyed in the collapse. Her office didn't have cameras and there was nothing left of the brief delivery of papers she'd gotten from Reese. They were probably ash at this point. All she had was the memory of his face, his voice, and whatever it was he'd done to heal himself in front of her eyes.

That last part wasn't something she was going to tell anyone just yet. Given her own method of calamity survival, it wasn't outside the realm of reason that other people could have unusual abilities too. It's just that she'd never encountered them before. She didn't heal, though. She just disappeared.

She'd called a friend at the Oklahoma City Police Department once things had settled down. She arranged to spend time with a sketch artist and tried to get as much as possible of Reese's face down on paper for herself. Maybe she could find him some day but, given the dead-ends she'd hit so far, it probably wasn't going to be any time soon. There wasn't a good way for her to quickly search Oregon's DMV records, even if they let her, without just sitting down and looking at every licensed driver in his rough age, height, and weight ranges. That was going to require a lot of time and, even then, it wasn't going to be too easy to convince them to let her, or even her office, have access to their database. She worried this was going to take her a while.

2014, October 2nd, Thursday Morning

Luckily for Hani, there was a coffee shop just south of Glisan on 13th, right across the street from the UPS Store where Robert McBride got his mail. She was worried this wasn't going to succeed. He might not pick up his mail today, tomorrow, or Saturday. She was seriously considering calling in sick until she'd found this guy. He must pick up his mail at least once a week, right? What if someone else picked up his mail for him?

Hani was surprised at the amount of traffic through the store. Men, women, old, young. People with dogs, people with babies. She'd always figured places like this only had serious patronage around Christmas time or something. A few guys gave her a start, but had various deal-breaking features. For a while she worried about beards or glasses, or baseball caps. If he had all three, she'd probably miss him entirely.

The morning slid by, and Hani was getting seriously caffeinated. Around noon, she switched to fruit juice to complement her tiny fancy sandwich. She wished there was a grocery store nearby but this area of the city looked like eating at home was discouraged. She had tilted her head back for the last of her drink when she saw him.

Reese/McBride was walking down the opposite side of the street and pulled open the door to the UPS Store. Hani realized she was frozen with an empty bottle held over her mouth. She put it down slowly and carefully picked up her bag. With a quick glance at traffic, she trotted across the street and stood in front of the UPS Store. She could see him inside going through a small stack of mail.

The beginning of Ghostbusters flashed in her mind. "So whadda we do?" Venkman asks his stunned compatriots after they see their first ghost.

"We've gotta make contact—" Hani recited to herself under her breath. She never really thought this day would come. She consciously straightened up, put on a friendly smile, and sucked in her breath as he approached the door. The door swung open and he stepped out. It was unmistakably him.

"Excuse me," Hani started. "I'm not a threat to you."

Reese/McBride looked up, half confused and half annoyed.

Hani continued, "We met at the bombing in Oklahoma. You introduced yourself as Carl Reese, and I've been trying to find you ever since." Great job, not stalkery at all, she thought, mentally rolling her eyes at herself.

She'd expected surprise, but instead his eyes went very cold. He looked past her to the other side of the street, and then up and down the block, "I don't know what you're talking about."

This wasn't going to work. She had to be totally honest, "I'm like you, but different. Neither of us could have survived the blast. I saw you heal, and I don't know what you saw of me, but I know you were looking at me when the room collapsed. Both of us should be dead."

* * *

Rob finished scanning the windows and rooftops and then looked back at this woman standing in front of him on the street. She held his gaze. She looked very much like the woman from

Oklahoma. She'd worked for the government then, though. Was there a SWAT team around a corner? It seemed extremely unlikely this was anything other than what she was saying it was. If some organization had found him, they wouldn't confront him like this. He'd probably just wake up in a cell. He didn't remember all the details of that morning in Oklahoma but a lot still stood out. Her last name he'd remembered, and her flickering. Other details eluded him at the moment. It was all in one of his journals, though. He broke the uncomfortable silence, "Ms Gittel, yes?" He could see the emotion in her eyes.

"Yes. You remember, then?"

"Yes. This ... isn't what I was expecting to be doing today. Will you walk with me?" Rob asked. She nodded, and he started walking away from his home. He wasn't coming up with many private places to talk. Maybe the riverfront would be reasonable. How much did she know? How had she found him?

"Please call me Hani," she said. "I do want to stress that I mean you no harm. I just want to understand what happened." She paused, looking pained, "Should I call you ... McBride? Reese?"

Rob really didn't like this, but he was going to have to roll with it, "I'm Rob here. How did you find me?"

"I've spent the last twenty years trying to track down the threads of your life as Carl Reese. The Oregon DMV never wanted to let me paw through their photo database on my own and I wasn't able to find anyone at the FBI to take an interest in helping me find you," Hani explained.

Rob wasn't sure if he should be more or less concerned. If this had been anyone else, he would have bolted and started to burn down this identity. "I'm vaguely relieved, I guess."

Hani continued, "Earlier this year, it came to my attention that

Oregon was working on a facial recognition project with the FBI, trying to link DMV records up with federal databases. I got to know the folks involved and set out to see if I could get a photo of you. It took me most of last month to find a photo of you in Eugene. I exhausted several newspaper archives, but I managed to find one picture. With that, I was able to find you here in Portland."

Rob eyed her. Twenty years. She was not messing around. He asked, "And you never told anyone about what you saw?"

"No. I've had plenty of experience with people not believing me about the thing that I do, so I never even considered trying to tell anyone what I saw you do in Oklahoma City. I had to be careful with my *own* situation there," Hani explained.

Rob was pretty confused about what he'd seen. It had been hard to make out between the debris, the flames, and the concrete collapsing on his head. It never sat right with him but he'd just written it off as an artifact of a massive, if temporary, concussion. He asked, "Clearly, you've surprised me. This isn't meant as rude, but ... what do you want?"

Hani considered this for a moment and said, "I want to understand what you can do and what you are. I don't entirely understand my own condition. I just know that ... I ... can't be killed. And I saw you regenerate half your body. Do you just heal quickly? I can get hurt. But anything life-threatening ... I just kind of avoid it. I've never had the nerve to test it, though. I don't want to be wrong."

Rob frowned, considering the situation. This was unique. Never in 700 years had he found anyone else able to cheat death. And she didn't even do it the same way.

Hani didn't wait for a reply, "I have so many questions."

They stopped to wait for a light before continuing their stroll toward the Willamette river. Rob was extremely nervous about trusting her, but it was clear she'd remembered what she saw. Rob said, "Well, you're not wrong about me. As far as I know, I cannot be killed. And I *have* tested it."

"What happened in Oklahoma City?" Hani asked. She had to know.

"Well, it's been a while. After the building collapsed, I healed again, but I was under a lot of debris. Since I was entirely unhurt, I was able to dig a little. It took a while but I got out by about midnight. The rescue efforts were focused in other areas. It was dark, and I wasn't injured, so I just walked back to my car and went back to my hotel, I think."

"You think?"

"I don't really remember all the details. I know I didn't stick around though. I abandoned my Oklahoma lay-over and continued on to Oregon. Seems like this entire mess can be tracked back to your office not getting a change-of-address form I mailed back in 1994," Rob smiled.

Hani nodded. "What about that? Why are you two people?"

"For now, let's say that it's something I do to help me stay unnoticed," Rob answered. They should probably stick to their shared experiences for now. Just because there were no black helicopters didn't mean he was safe.

"So you're not really Rob?"

"Well, I've been Rob a lot longer than I was Carl Reese. What about you? You don't have family to talk to about this?"

Hani looked sad for a moment and answered, "No, no one in my life. I have some friends, mostly coworkers at the Social Security Office, but no one I'd call close."

They arrived at the riverfront and found a vacant bench. They sat for a while in silence. Rob really had no idea what to do next. "So ... what should we do?"

Hani considered for a moment. "You had anyone you could show off your talents to?"

"For a while. But she didn't like it," Rob replied. He was a little surprised how easily he could talk to Hani. "I think it was a reminder of her mortality."

"Well, I want to see it. I'm not afraid," Hani said, furrowing her brow. "You said you'd tested yourself? I've spent years thinking what I saw was a dream. Show me."

2005, Spring

A steady glowing orb lit up the converted classroom, hovering above the test rig, drowning out the sunlight coming through the windows. Everyone held their breath.

"Almost there—"

The orb sputtered. Like the finale to a fireworks show, it crackled loudly and started throwing streamers. Some trickled across the ceiling, scorching the tiles. Others touched down at the edges of the rig. With a rush of air, the orb vanished, suddenly extinguished.

Dr Crawford Tillinghast looked around his lab. He peeled the safety goggles off his face as smoke curled up from the bank of refrigerator-sized capacitors at the far wall. "Is everyone okay?"

"Dammit," someone muttered from under the test rig table.

Crawford counted his graduate students as they emerged from their impromptu hiding places, sounding off in various states of surprise and disappointment.

"Jonesy, what happened?"

Jonesy turned back to her computer screen and studied the marching stream of information. "We were at 83 percent confinement when it looks like the capacitors stopped working."

"Stopped working? They're smoking!" another student unhelpfully offered.

Crawford slapped his clipboard to the ground. Papers popped

from the clip and splayed out at his feet. "These shitty capacitors—" he yelled to no one in particular "—are ruining everything!"

"Professor," Jonesy tried to interrupt.

"This could save the world," Crawford's voice cracked. He took a deep breath, and leaned down to pick up his clipboard and its spilled contents. Standing to face his slowly gathering PhD candidates, he took in their faces. This wasn't their fault. The manufacturing tolerances on the capacitors just weren't anywhere close to what they needed.

"*We* could save the world," he clarified. "This resonator could be installed in every neighborhood. This isn't just some experiment we're doing for fun here. I know you know that, but I just don't want you to get discouraged. It's just a matter of being able to get the resources to build the components we need to get it to scale up. We've seen it work in the small tests."

"Well, we've seen *something* happening in the small tests," Jonesy corrected.

"True, but I have faith. However briefly, we got out ten times the energy we put in. This is the brink of a new energy age, one where we're not bound by the costs of finding and burning fossil fuels, or the infrastructure expenses of hydro or wind power, or the inefficiencies of photoelectric. This has no consumables. This is self-sustaining, kids." Crawford looked around, trying to win them back over.

"More like self-destructive," Jonesy suggested. "I hope you're right, Professor. I want you to be right. I want us to figure this out, it's just that we don't have the equipment we—"

The smoking capacitors burst into flames, engulfing the back wall of the lab.

* * *

Crawford pushed open the door to the Regent's office. He tried to ignore the shiny leather chairs and immaculate mahogany desk he was approaching. How much further along could his work be now if he'd had the same budget they'd used on this office? He put on a smile, walked boldly to a chair, and greeted the Regent cheerfully, "Good afternoon, Dr Markham!"

"Dr Tillinghast, yes. Please have a seat," the University's Regent motioned for Crawford to sit down.

Crawford tried to direct the conversation right away. "I trust you're moving us to better labs on campus?"

Markham stared at Crawford for several seconds, sighed, and lifted some papers from an open notebook on his desk. "You nearly burned down a building, Dr Tillinghast."

"The fire department was able to contain it. Surely insurance has covered the damages?"

Markham flipped through the papers. "You have been working on your energy system for almost three years now. In that time, you have run up huge equipment bills, knocked out campus electricity four times, blown out windows in two separate labs, and last week you caught your entire lab on fire which spread to the floor above."

"We've always cleared our safety inspections. Certainly you're not trying to say we're delinquent in our preparations?" Crawford grasped for excuses.

"That's true," Markham admitted, "but for us to keep our insurance, we've had to exclude you from coverage."

"What does that mean, exactly?"

"It means you can't run a lab at the University anymore."

Crawford stared blankly at Markham for a few moments. He

gathered his emotions, and tried again. "This is important work we're doing. This could change the course of humanity. Millions, maybe billions, would suddenly have light, clean water, transportation. This energy source is like nothing the world has seen before. We could—"

"Professor Tillinghast," Markham interrupted, "the Board just isn't able to keep paying for these experiments. After last week's incident—"

"We can save lives! No one has to go to war, no one has to die over gold, or diamonds, or oil ever again!" Crawford was getting red in the face.

Markham studied Crawford for several seconds. "When I started as Regent, my predecessor filled me in on you, Professor. He said you were a man of conviction. He said your work on quantum mechanics was unparalleled."

Crawford shifted in his seat uncomfortably.

"He also said," Markham continued, "that when you lost your son, you became haunted. You started your energy production research, and were never the same again."

"Don't bring my son into this," Crawford said flatly.

"I'm sorry, I mean no disrespect, and I'm sorry to even mention it," Markham paused, trying to find the right words. "Look, I know you're a driven and gifted individual. I want you to stay with this University. Your students love you, and you are a strong mentor. If you can let the energy research go, and come back to working on physics, or really anything at all, I can make it happen."

Crawford took a deep breath. "But if not, I'm out?"

"My hands are tied." Markham closed the notebook in front of him. "We want you to stay, but your current research is too costly."

"What about the students on the project with me?"

"We've arranged for them to join other projects. Well ... all except one, who refused reassignment." Markham opened the notebook again and scanned the contents. "Joan Shelby."

Crawford smiled. "Jonesy," he said quietly to himself.

"What?" Markham leaned slightly forward.

"Thank you, Dr Markham. I'll consider what you've said," Crawford lied. He stood up, shook Markham's hand, and retreated from the office.

He started the short walk to the faculty parking structure and tried to imagine what it would take to set up an off-campus lab. They were going to need more than just a room for the test rig. For this to move forward, he was going to need to get into the capacitor manufacturing business. Without a clean and, more importantly, robust energy source to jump start the resonance, there was no way forward with his research.

He unlocked his car and got in. He steered his way through the parking garage and out onto the streets that snaked through the University campus. Ellen would be home by now. He'd have to convince her that it made sense to put a second mortgage on the house. Between that and the credit cards, he would have enough to get the ball rolling on the new lab. Since this was operating outside the confines of the University, he'd be the sole owner, so he could license the technology. Once they had shown a strong resonance effect, he'd be able to pay everything back.

Jonesy would be his sole assistant, at least for a while. Maybe he could get some non-military grants or investments and hire more people. Crawford almost missed his own driveway, pondering the different roles he wanted to fill in the new lab.

He pulled up behind his wife's car under their carport, shut off the engine, and got out. Their house wasn't huge, but it had a lot of equity. Ellen's parents had helped them buy it after they first got married. They'd been very generous, and he was glad they hadn't lived to see their grandson go off to war.

He let himself in and dropped his keys on the stand near the front door. The keys slid to a stop next to the small picture of his son, standing proudly in the Iraqi desert with an assault rifle hanging across his chest. He saw that picture every day as he left, and every night when he came home. After he was done, no child would ever have to die again over the government's obsession with cheap oil.

2014, October 2nd, Thursday Afternoon

Rob decided to just dive in. It seemed totally impossible that this was some elaborate effort to trap him. His residential address wasn't tied to McBride's financial foot-print, but if someone wanted to find it, they'd just have to follow him. There wasn't any need for a trick with Hani. And besides, he remembered her from Oklahoma City. He suggested relocating to his condo and she didn't hesitate.

On the walk back to the Pearl, they talked about the ways he passed the time. "Right now, a lot of walking. I'm mostly just trying to burn as much time as possible. My plan since the 50s has been to try and build a financial network that can support me. In theory, enormous money should be able to buy me true isolation. I don't want to turn into some kind of lab rat."

Hani nodded, "Makes sense. How long have you been alive?"

"Over half a millennium," Rob answered with a grin. "It's taken me a long time to figure out what I want to do when I grow up. And it hasn't all been clear sailing. One thing that I don't seem to have is superhuman memory. So much of my life is lost to me. Times where things just kind of happened without event didn't really stick with me."

"I can't decide if that's sad or a relief for you," Hani said.

Rob frowned a bit. "Yeah, me either, really. What about you? You don't seem much older from when I saw you in Oklahoma. Different hair, maybe?"

"Oh, you noticed," Hani joked, pushing her hair over an ear. "Well, yeah. I don't have much of an explanation. Everyone's always assumed I'm younger than I am. When I sat down and calculated it out, I think I'm aging at about half speed. I, uh, fudged my own records at the Social Security office, actually."

They'd reached his condo. Rob put in the door code and they walked through the lobby to the elevators. He pressed "10" and they waited. Rob took the moment to look carefully at Hani. She looked maybe late 30s, probably early 40s. She seemed to be in good shape—their walk across the city and back hadn't slowed her down at all. He'd had several lifetimes of common sense, so he nervously offered, "I'd guess mid-30s?"

Hani grinned. The elevator went "ding", and they got in. After the doors shut, Hani took in a big breath and said, "I'm 76."

Rob's eyebrows went up. "Wow, very cool. You don't look a year over 60!" He flashed her a smile. "No wonder you needed to get a job with the Social Security Administration. I hope no one ever investigates *you*!"

Hani crooked up a corner of her mouth, pleased with herself. "I really try not to give them a reason. I guess I was so taken with your financial trail because it looked so much like my own in a way. I've changed offices twice now. After ten or fifteen years, I was worried my coworkers would start to notice. I had just started at the Oklahoma City office at the end of 94."

"And you reset your history each time? Heh, good call. I've taken to building identities and stepping into them when they become age-appropriate for me. That has worked smoothly, except for Reese. That whole thing was a mess," Rob said. "I just wanted to see some bears in Yellowstone."

They stepped out on the 10th floor. "This is me. I've got a neighbor at that end, and I'm in 101 on the other half of the floor," he said, pointing toward his door. "I'm hoping I can buy them out when they leave. I'd rather have the entire floor to myself."

He let them in and gave Hani a quick tour. Through his front door was the main hall; coat closet on the left. At the end of the short hall, his kitchen opened out to the left. Beyond it was the half bath. Next to that, his office, which he skimmed over quickly—the journals could wait until later. Walking back and around to the right of the front hall was the main room with the huge windows looking out over downtown Portland. Past that was his master bedroom with the master bath beyond it. He came back around and ended the tour in the kitchen. "You want anything? A drink? Snack?" He pulled a glass out of a cabinet for some water for himself.

Hani eyed the glass of water and asked, "I could use something a lot stronger."

"Wine?" Rob offered.

"Yeah, I could go for a nice red," Hani confirmed.

Rob turned, pulled a wine goblet from its hanging rack, and walked across to the pantry. "What century?"

"Oh shit, I didn't mean—" Hani looked flustered.

"Hah, no worries. I'm only kidding. Most of the really old stuff I've got somewhere else. How about a nice Zin from 2009?" Rob plucked the bottle from its shelf and started opening it.

"That sounds great, thanks," Hani said. "Sorry, I'll be right back. I drank a *lot* of coffee waiting for you this morning. Bathroom's down on the left?" Hani started down the hall without waiting for an answer.

"Yup." Rob filled her glass and set it on the counter as Hani disappeared into his bathroom. He felt comfortable with her here, which was strange considering he rarely had guests. His environment had been carefully tuned for a serious bachelor lifestyle. And not the kind of bachelor that had frequent novel guests; he didn't make a habit of entertaining.

He thought for a moment and then pulled a black cutting board out from its home next to the sink and set it on the kitchen island. He fished around under the counter and came up with a gallon size zip-lock bag which he opened and carefully placed next to the cutting board. Finally, he reviewed his cutting knives. Probably best to do this quick. He plucked out his largest butcher knife, and set it next to the cutting board, on the side opposite the baggie.

Hani returned. "Okay, so much better." She noticed his preparations and started to look worried.

"Alright," Rob picked up the wine glass and handed it to her. "Drink up. You wanted a demo? Let's get this done."

A twinge of realization flashed across Hani's face. She looked up from the cutting board to Rob, then took the wine glass from him and downed its entire contents. "Whoooh. Okay. Mm, huh, that's good stuff. Okay ... go."

Rob picked up the blade, set his left hand down on the cutting board, and took in a deep breath. "I may be immortal, but this shit really hurts still."

Hani reflexively cringed but kept her eyes open. This was not the time to look away.

Rob swung down with all his might and severed his wrist. There was a surprising amount of blood and he let out a choked grunt. The knife blade was pushed out of the way as a new hand bubbled out of his wrist. It made an audible popping noise and bones stitched themselves together with ligaments and tendons. No more than a second later, the pain was gone and he turned to wave his new fingers at Hani. He had to remind himself to let go of the butcher's knife still in his other hand. His knuckles were white from the grip.

Hani stared, her mouth open slightly. Her face was a strange combination of wonder and relief. Rob had never seen that reaction before. It was always fear or disgust or both.

"Ho. Lee. Shit," Hani gasped. She picked up the Zinfandel bottle and poured herself another glass.

Rob cleared the cutting board of his prior hand into the zip-lock bag. It was still draining blood. "I'll need to do more than compost this. Law enforcement doesn't tend to take too kindly to finding stuff like this."

"I bet!" Hani said, still wide-eyed. "I saw it before, but it's ... amazing to see it again. I spent so much time worried I'd just imagined what had happened. Nothing like that has ever accompanied my glitches."

"Glitches?" Rob rinsed the board off in his sink and took a sponge to his counter.

"That's what I've been calling it. I seem to just kind of skip over anything deadly. It feels like I'm on fast-forward. The world is tinged kind of gray and races by. When things are safe again, it stops. It's only been a handful of times, but it hasn't let me down yet," Hani paused. "Obviously." She grinned.

Rob grinned back. "And you're clearly not 76. And you don't heal fast?"

Hani pondered. "Well, I don't get sick often. I've broken bones, gotten cuts, etc. They seem to stick around. Nothing like yours."

Rob probed, "But maybe they heal faster than normal?"

"Maybe? I always just assumed I was impatient. Yours, though ... do you eat a lot?"

Rob dried his hands. "What?"

"You just generated an entire hand. The calories needed for that would be staggering. Are you hungry after that kind of thing?" Hani asked.

"Nope." Rob wasn't sure this was the best time to share his theories on how it worked. "I'm not really sure how it happens, but it always does."

"I wonder if there is some way we could leverage your abilities into free energy? A perpetual motion machine? I can't come up with anything that doesn't sound terrible for you though," Hani mused.

"Yeah. I could keep tossing my hands into a boiler fire. I think it'd work, but it'd hurt like hell and smell even worse," Rob joked. He'd considered similar ideas.

"I wonder if you could just donate blood forever?" Hani suggested. "That doesn't hurt past the pin-prick, right?"

"My body seems to ... reject the needle pretty quickly." Rob paused briefly. "What about you? Your situation doesn't lend itself to testing without taking quite a leap of faith," Rob pointed out.

"Well ... I've had it involuntarily tested a few times now," Hani started.

1983, Summer

Hani had known Linda since college. In '79, Linda moved to Montana with her man. They'd wanted to live off the land, not answer to anyone, and forge their own lives. The house was simple, old, but Tom kept it in working order. They had a relatively large garden, along with several chickens. They'd done pretty well keeping up with food, but they hadn't really gotten to their goal of being self-sustaining. They had plenty to eat during the summer and fall months, but they still had to visit the local market during the winter and spring months to fill gaps.

Over the last winter Linda had been writing Hani about their plans for moving up to some livestock, like a pig or two. She'd preferred getting some sheep but a neighbor (a term Hani found to be used rather loosely given the distances between houses) was selling some piglets cheap. Since the spring, though, the letters had gotten less frequent, and they were less excited. This was pretty uncharacteristic for Linda, who'd been a prolific and excitable correspondent for many years.

The letter that made Hani pack her bags and drive out to Montana was alarming. Linda had recounted how Tom had started drinking again, and how things were beginning to seriously deteriorate between them. Hani read between the lines and was concerned for her friend's safety. Linda and Tom didn't have a phone line so Hani just wrote a simple letter back saying she was headed to visit them. She suspected she'd beat the letter there, but it wasn't her fault they chose to be so off-grid.

The drive from Ohio took two very full days of driving. Hani camped in Minnesota and opted for a motel on the second night. She showed up on the morning of the third day.

"Knock knock!" Hani echoed as she rapped on the front screen door frame. The front door was open and Linda poked her head out from a room down the hall.

"Oh my god! Hani! What're you doing here?" Linda exclaimed. She came rushing down the hall, balling up an apron she'd just taken off. She opened the screen door, "Come in come in!"

"Hi!" Hani gave Linda a big hug. "I just couldn't wait to visit. I sent a letter, but I think I beat it here. I wish you had a telephone." Hani noticed a bruise on Linda's neck, mostly covered by the collar of her shirt.

"Oh, well, Tom doesn't want the interruptions," Linda tried to explain.

From the direction of the open back door came Tom's voice, "Linda! Who's there?"

Hani saw Linda flinch a little, like she'd forgotten Tom was even nearby. "It's Hani. She came to visit."

Tom stepped into the back doorway and paused to kick mud off his boots. "Oh. Hi Hani. Welcome to our little corner of the world."

They continued to exchange pleasantries and Linda suggested she and Hani drive in to town to get some extra things for lunch, more than what their garden had to offer. Tom objected at first, but ultimately relented after Linda suggested that they needed ice cream too.

On the way to the store, taking advantage of Tom not being

present, Hani tried to get a better sense of what was going on. "I saw your bruise."

Linda looked defensive. "It's nothing. He just gets too drunk sometimes. Money's been really tight and he hasn't been able to get a job."

Hani tried to convince Linda this wasn't a safe situation but Linda wouldn't listen. Hani dropped it for the moment and switched to gossiping about the lives of their former classmates.

They returned from grocery shopping a little after noon. Tom met them in the driveway and Hani could smell the whiskey before Linda had even turned off the engine. He seemed to be in mid-rant.

"—can't afford to feed ourselves, much less start taking in your good-for-nothing friends!" He shouted at no one in particular, while waving an empty glass around.

Linda stepped out of the car and tried to talk him down, putting a hand on his shoulder. "Tom, honey, it's barely noon, you can't—"

"Can't do what?! Drink?! I will do ... whatever I want." Tom swatted Linda's hand off him. "You don't tell me what to do. That's not how this works! Get back in there. Don't you have to make lunch for Hani here? Make lunch for the whole county!"

"Tom, please," Hani said, trying to redirect him.

Tom swiveled toward Hani. "She's very generous, you know that? Except with me. Right, Linda?" He turned back and shoved Linda toward the house. "Go on back inside!"

Linda stumbled to her knees and Hani darted between her and Tom. "Tom. You need to cool off."

Tom stared at Hani. "Trying to outnumber me, hunh? I'm done with this." He lumbered back to the house and disappeared inside with a slam of the screen door.

Hani helped Linda back up. "Are you okay?"

Linda was crying. "I wanted this to work so badly. If I could just get the open teaching job at the school, then I could—"

Tom banged back through the screen door. He'd replaced his empty glass with a revolver.

Well this escalated quickly, Hani thought to herself while trying not to totally panic. Linda stumbled away and fell back to the ground, eyes wide.

Tom started shouting, "I told you, Linda, you're worthless. Five years out here, and you just drain me. Get your friend outta here. There's no guest bedroom here."

Hani raised her hands and walked toward Tom. "Tom, look, I'll leave, just put—"

"You don't get to tell me what to do either!" Tom shouted and stuck the barrel of his gun in Hani's face.

"Tom, I'll do what you want. I'll leave." Hani said. "I can take Linda, and—"

Tom's eyes lit up with fury. "You'll take nothing." He pulled the trigger.

Hani saw the world flash gray for a fraction of a second and watched smoke trickle out of the gun barrel still held about two feet directly in front of her nose. The report echoed back to them from the mountains.

Tom looked confused. He squeezed his eyes closed and quickly opened them again.

Unsure of where Linda was behind her, Hani started to side-step towards her car, hoping to get Linda back in sight without looking away from Tom. Tom followed her with the gun, though he let it dip toward her chest. Hani could see Linda on the ground now. If Tom tried to move towards Linda, she'd be able to intervene.

"Shitty ammo," Tom mumbled and pulled the trigger again.

Hani briefly saw the gray tinted world again and heard glass tinkling to the ground behind her. Tom frowned. He emptied the revolver at Hani. On each blast, she could feel the world skip past her for an instant and she could hear her car absorbing the bullets behind her.

Tom clicked through a few empty chambers and then rubbed his eyes with his spare hand. Hani took the opportunity and closed the distance between her and Tom. Using her momentum, she carried through and drove her knee squarely into Tom's crotch and brought her heel down on top of his left foot. Tom howled in pain and took a sloppy swing at her with the revolver. She ducked and made her way over to Linda.

Linda was balled up, holding her head and sobbing.

"Up, come on, up, up," Hani ordered.

Linda looked up at her, shocked. Hani dragged Linda to her feet while keeping an eye on the now crouching Tom. Hani led Linda around to her passenger side door and guided her in.

Tom started growling as Hani made it to the driver's side. She opened the door and quickly swept glass from her seat. She dropped into her car and slammed the door shut as Tom began getting to his feet again. She started the engine up, drove around Tom and back out to the main road.

Linda never looked back.

* * *

Rob had listened intently to Hani's retelling. "So, just to clarify, you got shot point-blank, six times?"

"Well, they never hit me. It's more like I just fast-forward over the part where the bullets would have killed me," Hani said.

Rob pursed his lips. "What if he'd shot at your hand?"

"I think I'd be down a hand. I've gotten myself pretty hurt before. But anything serious, I just skip past," Hani replied, swirling wine around her glass.

"Have you tested it?" Rob asked.

"Tom was kind of a test. I mean, I was pretty sure he couldn't kill me, but it's not like it was a controlled environment. I just wanted to get Linda out of there."

"Yeah, absolutely." Rob considered things for a moment. "How about now, here? Gunfire might attract unwanted attention, but I've got an extremely sharp sword in my office. Want to demo your ability?"

Hani looked up from her wine at Rob. Her eyes wandered to the zip-lock bag and then back to Rob. "Probably the wine, but sure, I just spent twenty years trying to find you. What the hell else are we supposed to be doing?"

Rob nodded and got up, heading toward his office.

Hani yelled after him, "I swear to God, if this is some Highlander bullshit, I'm going to be seriously pissed off."

Rob returned with a samurai sword in hand. He pulled the sheath off and set it on the kitchen island. "I'll not go for your head. Good point about Highlander. I'm better with a long sword, but this is a bit more precise for stabbing. I can go for your heart, how about that?"

Hani held her gaze on the katana for a few seconds.

"If not, that's cool," Rob offered, starting to reach for the saya to sheath his sword.

"No, no, wait," Hani said, gesturing at him leave the saya where it was. "You know what you're doing?" Hani put her wine down on the counter.

"Yeah, I've trained," Rob assured her.

"Okay. Screw it. Go," Hani said, standing with her arms wide. "Just don't fuck this up."

Rob shifted his grip on the katana and stepped towards Hani. He set up his stance and tested the distance carefully. "You sure?"

"Yes. Do it before I chicken out."

Rob lunged forward and drove his weight out through his shoulder, stabbing at Hani's chest with his sword. There was a sharp popping noise, and Rob caught himself from falling forward. Hani was gone. He was standing about where she'd been. He backed up to where he'd started, keeping the sword level with where he'd expected it to land if there had still been a person with him in his kitchen. He let the sword drop to his side, which was immediately followed by a deeper popping noise as Hani reappeared exactly where she'd been.

"What'd it look like?" Hani asked, dropping her arms back to her sides.

"Shit, that's cool." Rob said. "You just vanished. When I stepped back, you reappeared."

"It's hard to really see it on my end. To me, it just looks like you moved really fast," Hani said. "But I know I did my thing because of the weird gray tinting of my vision when it happens."

Rob tried to collect his eyebrows from the top of his forehead. "I think we need to study what you can do; I know what I can do. I did the bulk of my research, if you could call it that, when I went by 'Leland' back in Britain."

1919, Spring

Marie had died in their London home on April 24th. She'd had the Spanish Flu and had been seen by all the doctors Leland could find. It was the pneumonia that they weren't able to keep up with. Leland could do nothing but sit by her side and hold her hand between coughing fits.

He always knew he'd see her die. She aged and he didn't. She had known about his condition for a decade already and she still married him. She'd always said he was her angel. She'd never wanted to know about his past, saying, "You're here with me now; I don't care how you got here." Perhaps she sensed there was a trail of blood behind him, or perhaps she just didn't want the reminder of her mortality.

They had just been starting to plan the rest of their life together when the War started. She'd insisted that he use his abilities to stop the Germans. She'd said, "Why else do you have this power? Make use of it. It's your God-given duty."

He'd wanted to stay with her. They could just slip away to the country and live life. Tea, horses, tiny sandwiches, sailing, anything but war and death and pain. Leland had sat, holding her hand as it cooled. So many people had died in the War. Everywhere he went, they were extinguished. And here now, home from the front, death waited for him again. Mocking his condition, making him watch as it plucked more souls from the innocent, the guilty, the young, and the old.

It had been a month since that night in their bedroom. She was in the ground now. The only person that had really known him. There wasn't a reason to keep going. It'd been close to 600 years of floating around the planet like some kind of bored ghost and here was the one love he'd found, gone. It was time to find a way to put an end to his travels.

The simple stuff didn't work, but he figured he'd try it all again. Maybe this time, he wouldn't heal. He'd prepared a couple new options, though. One was waiting for him just outside London. The construction was simple, it'd only taken a few days. The real trick was getting the blade out there on the train. The other option jingled in his pocket: six hand-casted silver bullets. He unlatched his steamer trunk and took out his service pistol and a big knife. The bayonet wasn't really going to help much here. He'd managed to sneak back a grenade as well. He filled a satchel with his weapons and walked out of their apartment. His apartment.

He knew the train schedule by heart, and he wasted no time getting to the station. The next train carried him to his destination: a little wooded area just outside the London city limits. The place he was thinking about was a short walk from the station. They'd spent many summer days exploring the trails.

After about an hour hike, he strayed from the trail into a small clearing. His machine was still there, covered in some fallen branches he'd arranged on it for camouflage, in case anyone had walked the same trails. It looked undisturbed. He'd try it last.

First, the grenade. Given his experiences in the War, he figured this was a waste of time. He walked away from the clearing and deeper into the forest. He hugged the grenade like a long-lost friend and pulled the pin. He counted the timer down out loud. "5... 4... 3... 2... 1..."

The forest shook from the impact. He only heard the echoes and the noises of birds taking flight. He was lying on his back, clothes shredded and bloodied. There was a small crater where he'd been standing, and the foliage in every direction had been painted red with his entrails.

He got up, and made his way back to the clearing. Time for the silver. This was supposed to kill werewolves, right? No soldier had ever fired silver at him before. He loaded the pistol and held it to his chest. He closed his eyes and collected his thoughts. He focused on Marie and put a bullet through his heart. He winced and felt his pulse skip a beat as muscle tissue reformed and continued on from its rude interruption. Maybe he needed a wooden stake instead.

He moved the gun to his forehead and hoped again. Pulling the trigger, his sight flashed white for an instant. The report had been cut short as his brain was unable to conduct information from his ears. But everything was rebuilt in an instant. He could hear his skull sliding back into place. The sensation was like cold sweat running up his forehead. It seemed silver was not the solution.

He reconsidered the wooden stake idea. He had a knife with him, so he wandered around the edge of the clearing looking for a decent candidate tree. About half-way around, he found one with a dead branch at the right height and with the right diameter. He took an hour to get it whittled it down to a point.

He backed up several paces and got himself ready. He sprinted at the tree, ignoring all his instincts to dodge out of the trunk's path, and instead impaled himself on the branch. It worked perfectly. He'd heard his ribs crack and his pulse stopped. He grinned while his vision started to collapse into a tunnel, but then felt the familiar sensation of his regeneration. His body exuded the branch and he fell backwards off the tree. He was going cold everywhere, but then he felt his pulse start back up.

Leland stood. Not a vampire either. But he'd known it wasn't going to work. It'd be too easy. It was time to lose his head. He pulled the branches from his hand-made guillotine and hauled it into an upright position. He fed the rope through the pulley at the top and tied it to the blade. He tested the blade channel. It had a sufficiently smooth action.

He had no reason to wait, so he lay down and pulled the blade up with a downward yank on the rope. He got comfortable and rolled onto his back. The sky was gray still, but it wasn't raining. Maybe this would be his last look at clouds. He let the rope go, and the blade skittered along its prescribed path. Leland could hear nothing, feel nothing. This was new.

There was a muffled rubbing noise, which quickly resolved itself into a wet pop and he could hear again. He blinked his eyes in the light. Same sky. He was half on and half off his guillotine bench. It seemed like his new head had shoved his body down away from the blade to make room for itself as it regrew. Leland walked around to the other side and was greeted by a perverse smile on his earlier face. His old eyes glared up at him, glassy.

He picked up his old head and pitched it into the forest, swearing after it. Not even a clean decapitation was going to solve his problem. He sat back down on the bench and held his new head in his hands. He cried.

He could still see her the day he'd left for the front. She was proud, she was beautiful. It was the last time he'd seen her so full of life. Why couldn't she regrow her lungs? Why couldn't he grow some for her. He could make spares of anything, everything. Even when he didn't want it. He wiped the blood from his face onto what was left of his pants and slid off the bench to the ground. He lay there, wishing for death, and watched the unfazed clouds flit past his gruesome auto-abattoir.

* * *

Rob poured himself a glass of wine, hoping to catch up to Hani's now two downed glasses. "Nothing can damage my body for long. In the 1990s, I borrowed a camcorder and set up some growth speed tests. It's one of the weirder things about my regeneration: it seems to take a constant time. It's just under three seconds."

Hani looked at the zip-lock bag. "Like just now? Your hand took about three seconds to grow back?"

"Right. But when I'd lop my arm off at the shoulder, it'd take the same time. The more there is to regrow, the faster that growth happens. I have no idea what it means. I wish it was faster though. The sensations from this are ... hard to adapt to. The pain followed by this rubbery numbness and then everything is back to normal. Somewhere on a list I'd wanted to see what in the world is happening to my endorphin and adrenaline levels. The pain dumps a ton of hormones into my blood stream, but they dissipate quickly. I don't remember ever going into shock."

Hani considered this for a while. "What about when you lose your head? It sounds like your neck coughs up a new head, rather than your head producing a new body."

"Yeah. Those are the worst. It's like experiencing nothing, except that it's much more disorganized. Like I either can't or won't think straight. There's no sensation, there's no real thought either, just a weird presence, like I'm aware of the fact that I'm alive and that's it." Rob fumbled trying to describe his headlessness.

"Sounds backwards to 'I think therefore I am.' More like, 'I am, therefore I think.'" Hani offered.

Rob smiled, "The thinking is not even really part of it. Just 'I am', and then I spend the rest of the time trying to remember what thinking is. I'm glad it's only a second." Rob gestured to the clock over the sink. "Been a long day of story telling. Shall we get dinner and talk about movies for a while? You can crash here if you want. We should get started in the morning."

Hani tilted her head a little, "Started?"

"Yeah, time for some science!" Rob exclaimed.

2014, October 3rd, Friday

Rob had driven Hani back to her hotel where she gathered her things and checked out early. He'd made up the couch and changed the sheets on his bed. Hani hadn't wanted to displace him from his bedroom, but he'd insisted. He was relatively unprepared for guests, but, in light of now having one, he'd wanted her to be comfortable. She'd relented and dragged her luggage into his bedroom, while Rob drew the blinds in the main room and settled onto the couch.

Hani woke to the sounds of shuffling, zippers, and other packing-related activities. She peeked outside the bedroom and saw Rob with several duffel bags in the main room. He was packing the sword from last night, along with several identical boxes. The other duffels were already zipped closed.

"Ah! Good morning, sorry if woke you. I got up early and was excited about what I think we can find out today." Rob was bright and animated.

Hani was not a morning person. In fact, his delight made her want to stab him in the eye, but she suspected it wouldn't be very satisfying.

"Do you drink coffee?" He asked.

"Yes," she managed to grunt.

"Great, I'll get it started," Rob said and wandered off to the kitchen.

Hani trudged back to her temporary bedroom and started

gathering her shower necessities. Twenty minutes and one hot shower later, she got dressed, and grudgingly headed out into the new day. At least it was being heralded by fresh coffee, to which she availed herself immediately.

"Okay, I'm feeling mostly human again," she said after she'd made her way through half her cup.

"Excellent!" Rob said. "Let's get all this stuff loaded up and head out. I want to try some things that aren't very compatible with walls or bystanders."

Hani raised an eyebrow and downed the last of her coffee. They lugged the bags to the elevator and carried them out to Rob's Jeep in the basement parking garage. Rob headed west out of the city. After about an hour, just east of the Tillamook State Forest, he turned north and started winding his way through farms that gave way to trees. Eventually they came to a stop at a dirt road with a heavy gate. He hopped out, gathered up the chain that was the keeping the gate shut and unlocked the padlock holding the bundle together. He swung the gate open, stepped back into the Jeep, drove through, and repeated the chain dance again, this time in reverse.

They continued down the path another mile and a small house came into view around a bend. He pulled up next to it and said, "This is it!"

Hani stepped out of the Jeep. "Does this place even have an address?" Hani asked, slamming her door shut.

"Nope! But it does have some electricity," he said, pointing up at the solar panels covering the roof.

"In Oregon? Are your solar panels rain-powered or something?"

"It's no Arizona, but with the batteries and hardly ever spending time here, it does just fine," Rob said with mock defensiveness.

"Alright. So what's the big secret? What've you got planned for us?" Hani inquired, dropping the last of the duffel bags on the house's porch.

"First ... breakfast!" Rob unzipped the duffel closest to him and pulled out several plastic containers and some cutlery. "I made us some biscuits and gravy to go."

"You're frustratingly productive in the morning," Hani observed.

They sat on the porch. The meal was amazing. Seems like being immortal for 700 years had some additional advantages in the food preparation department. She finished her meal and stuffed the Tupperware back in the duffel it had come from.

"Okay, Hani," Rob said, "I want to get a couple things done. As part of it, I'm just going to leave a camera running since I think you've never seen your own displacements."

"Yeah, cool."

Rob extended the legs on a tripod he'd produced from the heavier duffel and set up his video camera. "I'm still impressed by humanity's progress in this department. We've really come a long way on technology. It still feels like magic to me and I've had the chance to watch it develop over the centuries. I'm still disappointed in the way things turned out for Nikola Tesla. Almost everything he designed is in active daily use everywhere in the world, but he died broke. I hope he had a sense of what kind of impact he'd had."

"Yeah, I'd read a bit about him recently. Hasn't his stuff been mostly unchanged?" Hani asked. She stood up, brushing some pine needles off her pants.

"For the most part. No one has really improved any of it. It's been a century, and high voltage power transmission is still mostly the way he designed it. His work on wireless communication, though, has been extensively expanded," Rob mused. "Okay, I'm almost ready. Let's start with the sword again, but I want to add some elements to the test. One second." Rob ran to the house and came back with a kitchen stool.

Rob had Hani stand about 15 feet from the camera, half-facing it. He gathered a few wet pine cones from the ground, and handed them to her, "Set these in your hands, palm up, fingers open."

Hani stood with her pine cones while Rob unpacked his katana. He set it on the stool next to him.

"Ready?" he asked, positioning himself arms-length from Hani.

"Yup, go for it," Hani confirmed. She glanced at the camera and then back to Rob.

Rob started high up for a slash instead of a stab. This would make it easier for him to control his momentum when she vanished. He set up to chop down through her neck towards her sternum. On execution, she audibly popped out of existence and the pine cones dropped to the ground. Rob shook his head, still not used to this. He held the sword where Hani had been and reached back for the stool, dragging it forward. He placed it where she'd been standing and rubbed his ears. It felt like maybe he'd done (and healed) damage to his hearing. Perhaps her displacement of air was louder than he realized.

With the stool in place, he pulled the sword back and set it aside. He checked the camera and then his watch. He waited for a few minutes, then went back to the stool and lifted it to move it out of the way. As he turned with it, he felt a small blast of air and felt a deep thump as Hani reappeared.

"Was that longer?" Hani asked.

"Yeah, I blocked you with the stool," Rob said, pointing at it. "I waited about 5 minutes. The moment I moved it out of your way, you came back. Here, check out the footage."

As they watched the playback, a little smile started to develop on Hani's face. "That's cool. I guess I didn't consider the air around me. From the movement of the grass and leaves it looks like I just leave a vacuum? I wonder how I push air out of my way on the way back."

"We should get a high-speed camera. On the frame-by-frame, it looks like you're just back instantly. Weird. I'd expect it to heat your skin … or cool it? I'm not really sure," Rob said.

"It doesn't feel like anything, really. There's no sound at all. What I see is weird, though."

"You want to get displaced for longer? I could park the Jeep in the way, or pile up some wood?"

"No, I don't entirely enjoy the weird state. Reminds me too much of the first time."

"Cool, no worries; we've got plenty more stuff to try. What about continuous action? We've only tried this with you standing still. What if you're running at me and I'm shooting at you? Does it interrupt your momentum?" Rob wondered.

Hani furrowed her brow and replied, "I think it's unchanged, based on some other stuff I've been through."

Rob nodded. "In that case, I wonder how you deal with falling?"

Hani frowned. "I'm not sure about that."

"Well, we'll come back to it. Let's get momentum on tape first."

"On 'tape'?" Hani grinned.

"Disk! 'Recorded'? I have no idea what you kids call it these days," Rob waved his hand mock-dismissively. He dug around in the nearest duffel and came out with a box of ammo and a handgun. He unlocked it and loaded the magazine. He had Hani back up while he reset the camera.

"Okay," Rob said, taking a shooting stance. "Run at me!"

Hani galloped toward him and he fired. Nothing connected and he could barely see her vanishing. The cracks from the gun were augmented with a weird puffing noise coming from Hani's near-instantaneous displacements. She came panting up to him as the slide on the pistol locked back, magazine empty.

"Well, okay, no problem with momentum there!"

Hani braced herself on her knees, "I don't run a lot."

Rob grinned. "I'd like to try something else: fire," Rob suggested, pointing to the gas canister on the back of the Jeep.

"Fire?"

"Yeah. You ditched the pine cones, so I wonder if you can do the same with a liquid. I'd like to start with water, first, though, since I don't want this going wrong."

"Yeah, let's do water and go from there," Hani said. She'd gotten burned on stoves and plenty of other things, so this didn't sound entirely great to her.

Rob nodded and wandered off to the house again, this time coming back with a pan filled with water and a book of matches. "Ready?" he asked after starting the camera again.

"Screw the ice bucket challenge," Hani muttered. "Go for it."

Rob dumped the pot of water over her shoulders and then picked up the sword for another slash. The water had soaked into her clothes and hair.

"Shit that's cold" Hani cringed.

"Sword?" Rob confirmed.

"Go."

He stabbed at her and she cracked out of the world, leaving the water to sprinkle across Rob's arms. On withdrawing the sword, she appeared with a thump. She was dry.

"You're dry." Rob offered. He deferred thinking about the fact that she took her clothes with her when she displaced.

"Well that's cool."

"Literally?" Rob checked.

"Well, a little, but not as cold as the water itself," Hani considered.

"Yeah, I guess ... you're evaporating, not the water? I really don't know what we're dealing with here," Rob tried to remember all the physics he'd learned over the ages. "Gasoline?"

"Sure, let's do it," Hani said.

Rob fetched the gas canister and spun the cap off. "Ready?"

"Okay to go," Hani said, closing her eyes.

Rob dumped gas out at her feet and then up her front and back. He set the canister to the side, and lit a match. He tossed it at her and she popped away just before the match would have reached her. Her wake, however, sprayed gas everywhere, catching the match in midair, igniting their clearing in a giant fireball.

Rob and the camera were blown back. Rob's clothes and face were on fire. "Ow, shit," he narrated as he rolled on the ground, trying to put out his pants. The flames were snuffed on him and his vision cleared as dead skin flaked off his face and hands, evicted by the replacements. The camera was okay, so he propped it back up and surveyed the clearing. The center was still engulfed with a healthy blaze. He ran back to the house and returned with the extinguisher he kept by the wood stove.

A few blasts of retardant and Hani snapped back into the clearing, pushing the white mist away from her.

"Woo, that was weird," Hani said, rubbing her shoulders.

"You okay?" Rob verified.

"Yeah, I'm fine. Gasoline on my skin just feels kinda terrible, but that went away. What happened?"

"Well … I hadn't considered the effect of your vanishing. It kind of sprayed the gas everywhere, aerosolized it quite a bit more than I'd expected. I think I grew a new face," Rob smiled, exercising his new cheeks.

They reviewed the recording. Hani watched the frame by frame and noticed what Rob had suspected. "I didn't even catch fire."

"Yeah, there's some kind of threshold that gets crossed and you leave. And this time you didn't come back until all the fire was thoroughly out," Rob noted.

"I missed the explosion entirely."

1917

The howitzers had been raining artillery on them all morning. So far, Leland had found the Western Front in France to be a miserable experience. No one noticed his knack for being able to "dodge" bullets when he spent time surveying the no-man's land between the trenches. When gunfire started, everyone else ducked, so no one had seen him repeatedly rebuilding his face. The German snipers were pretty accurate.

The actual rain had stopped earlier in the morning. This made reconnaissance much easier. After the last facial reconstruction, he'd gotten a good look at the sniper position on this side of the ridge. Leland yelled, "Mack, grenade!"

Private Mack peeked around the trench corner and lobbed a grenade at Leland, leaving the trigger pin in place. Leland held the spoon down and pulled the pin. He stuck his head up and back down again, seeking to avoid the now common sting of a bullet popping his skull open. He let the spoon fly from the grenade, counted to two and pitched his gift at the sniper's nest. A dull thump followed by silence seemed like a pretty successful toss.

"I think that's got him," Leland yelled back over his shoulder. Six of his team rounded the corner, rifles slung around their bodies.

"Should we go over the top here?" Mack asked, "It looked like most of the barbed wire was down on their side."

Leland nodded, "I think we've got a—" He suddenly found it

tricky to take a breath and noticed the tip of a bayonet protruding from his chest. His friends' eyes were wide with surprise. Some had managed to get their rifles unslung and start firing as they retreated down the trench. Others closer to the front got cut down by the Germans who'd made similar observations about the state of the barbed wire. The bayonet sharply dislodged itself.

Leland watched as Mack was hit by a bullet and slumped to the side of the trench. His cheek left a streak along the mud wall as he pitched forward, lifeless. Leland reached for his side arm and felt a few bullets rip through his arm. He grimaced and turned, staring at his the new assailants. They fired a few more times. One managed to clip him just below his jaw. Leland felt his head tilt slightly and rebound as muscles wrapped back around his neck. He growled and started firing into the Germans.

They dropped one after another. He ran out of ammo as he approached the last of them who was shrieking and swearing at him. His German had gotten rusty, but he could make out "devil" and "cursed." Leland picked up a fallen rifle and prepared to impale the final interloper with its bayonet. Instead, the soldier spat at him and held a grenade out, glaring at Leland as it exploded.

As Leland's brain reassembled itself, he began to feel the mud he was lying in. His vision returned and he watched the thin clouds scoot by in the sky for a few moments. The adrenaline had already receded, but he couldn't shake the image of Mack smearing his dead face through the mud. Leland stood up and turned around to find several of his unit gaping at him.

"That ... isn't possible," Private Finn stammered.

Leland shrugged and said, "I just got lucky, that Kraut accidentally shielded me from the blast."

"No ... no he didn't. That's your leg," Finn insisted, pointing at a boot holding a bloody stump that lay between the two of them in the mud. "You're ... unharmed."

The other surviving soldiers stared. Leland sighed. This might be a problem but he was too pissed about Mack to hide his condition anymore.

"God has saved you Leland! You've been saved!" Finn demanded.

The rain started back up.

"God has cursed me, Finn," Leland corrected. He ditched the rags of what was left of his uniform and started rolling one of the fallen German soldiers over to exchange clothes. "Finn, can you give me my boot back? I've had enough of this. Can you guys collect all the grenades you can?"

Finn stood, motionless, watching Leland drag the German coat from the body. Leland pondered the new jacket for a moment and then gave up on it. He was unlikely to stay particularly well-clothed if this went the way he was planning.

Leland dropped the jacket and looked up, snapping his fingers in Finn's face. "Finn, get it done. This isn't a surprise to me. I know what I am."

Finn's eyes focused on Leland again and he stammered, "You ... you've known this whole time? You have to save us! Get us out of here, Leland, please! They're going to kill us all!" Artillery exploded nearby, driving home Finn's pleas.

"Yes, I know. I was hoping to just help. I've been down this path before and it doesn't turn out well for me," Leland intoned.

Several of the other soldiers came back with a few grenade belts. Leland collected a half dozen of the Germans' rifles and threw them over his shoulder. He gathered the grenade belts and said, "Get the others. Tell them what you've seen. I'm going over the top. I want you guys to follow in about five minutes. I'm going to need a lot of grenades. And ammo. Your job now is to not get shot and to resupply me."

They nodded at him. Each had a confused look of surprise, terror, and hope. The hope was new. Leland worried the terror was about him too, though, but shook it off, turning back to the trench wall. He climbed up, taking several bullets to the face and shoulders. He dragged the belts behind him, hoping to shield them with his body.

It was like walking through a strong wind. Every step he took was interrupted by lost bone, muscle, and blood. He was frequently off balance, losing the coherence of his joints, or having his legs snap from under him. He kept picking himself up, trying to meditate on the pain and cool numbing sensation of his regenerating body. There were brief moments of reprieve as the forward German trench reloaded. He made reasonable progress and, as he neared the other side, he could hear the chatter of fearful alarm from his enemies.

He pulled up a grenade and lobbed it into the trench ahead of him. Mud and flesh sprayed up out of the trench with a thunderous pop. The vantage point from above the trenches was much better, but progress was exhausting. He let himself down into the trench and prepared a rifle in one hand and a grenade in the other. At each corner, he tossed a grenade, waited, and rounded the corner to pick off the survivors.

One intrepid German managed to gore Leland as he came around the corner. Leland felt the tip scratch across his spine from the inside and started to grunt from the pain. Instead, he turned it into a shrill laughing battle cry. He threw the soldier to the ground and pulled the rifle away from his body.

"This war is done," he hissed at the terrified teenager. Leland stabbed him through the eye, and continued forward, sick with himself but unwilling to give this up. Too many of his friends had fallen. This conflict was worse than anything he'd seen before. The scale of it.

Leland's compatriots called to him from around the prior corner, "How's ammo holding up?"

"I'm good for the moment. Stay back," Leland replied.

He cleared several more trenches. His uniform was almost entirely shredded at this point. His helmet hadn't made it past the initial attack. He'd lost his other boot at some point on this side and he was about to be exposing himself to his enemies soon if he didn't watch out. Or maybe that shock might give him an additional advantage.

Around the next corner, someone deflected his grenade up and out of the trench. They rushed him around the corner and several stabbed at him with their bayonets. Most connected. Those that missed pulled back and tried again, until he was on his back, skewered like he'd fallen into a pit of spikes. He growled at them.

They shot him in the face several times. He continued his growling and while one reloaded, managed to sneak in some curses, "I'm just waiting for you to run out of ammo." One seemed to understand English and began urging the others to stop shooting. They watched him repairing his face for the hundredth time today. As he lay there, he could feel his body chewing away at the steel of the bayonets. He felt one snap, and the soldier withdrew his rifle, examining the place where most of his bayonet had been.

Leland used the moment to flick a pin from the grenade he'd had readied. "Enjoy hell, boys," he spat at them as he counted the grenade down. At five seconds in, he produced it from them to see, and bounced it up into the air a little, closer to their faces. The world flashed to white, and the explosion was cut short by his nervous system suddenly lacking structure.

He became sensate again, as before: lying in the mud, watching the sky roll past him. Part of the wall behind him had collapsed. The mud was sticky with blood. He was inured to the spray of body parts around him, his own included. His team rounded the corner.

"I think I'm out of rifles," Leland announced.

"Leland, you okay?" Finn yelled.

"Yeah, just give me a second," Leland said, sitting up. He surveyed this portion of the German trench system and noticed one of his enemy was slumped near a wireless telephone station. "I think we've been found out," he said, pointing to the station. The others nodded in understanding and pulled up their gas masks. They all cocked their heads to listen for bombers. The day was starting to run out, and it was relatively quiet.

"Well, I think we should get out of here," Leland said, looking around for pants that might fit him.

"Sir, pants," Finn offered. "Private Jenkins suspected you might need some clothes and has been collecting as we went."

"Thank you. And I'm a Private too, why the 'sir' stuff?"

Finn raised an eyebrow and said, "I have no idea what to call you. You're some kind of angel, but 'sir' seemed appropriate. I could try 'your holiness', if you want."

"Ugh, no, no. I'm still one of you. I'm just … resilient," Leland resisted.

"You can call it anything you want, Sir. You're a killing machine, sent to save our asses." Finn tipped his helmet back and wiped his forehead.

"Well, we're going to run out of ammo eventually. Can any of you drive a tank?"

1975

Moving was a difficult choice to make. With her friends getting older and having families, it was starting to stand out that Hani wasn't aging like they were. She didn't want to have to explain it to them, but it was hard to sever those connections. Not like she could really explain it to them since she didn't understand it herself.

She'd not stayed in contact with the couple of other children at the orphanage who had seen her one event there. Of the friends she'd made in college, and since then, she hadn't told many about her time at the orphanage. None of them knew her history further back.

With over ten years since graduating from Oberlin, she'd built a decent life for herself. With all her makeup off, and no fashion to assist her, she looked like she was in her early twenties. She tried to keep up with everyone else, but most of her friends from her graduating class were 37 this year. She felt 37, but she didn't look it. Instead of continuing this path, she got herself a transfer to North Platte, Nebraska.

Most of her apartment contents were in a truck somewhere on the road behind her. Her back seat and the trunk were filled with the essentials. She wasn't looking forward to spending the night in a sleeping bag on the floor in her new place, but the schedule really wasn't working out well and she couldn't afford to stay in a motel until the truck unloaded everything. She'd had to dip into savings to pay for the moving company but, after her calculations, it was cheaper than just re-buying everything in Nebraska.

What a change from Ohio and from Massachusetts. At least in Ohio she'd been in a college town, but there was little for her in Massachusetts. She'd gotten out of there as soon as she could. The orphanage hadn't been terrible, but it hadn't been fun, either. High school was tricky because she was so little, compared to the other girls. Somehow, no one seemed to really think it was of note, but she wrote that off to her having continued from the orphanage to high school with many of the same kids. Perhaps her orphanage stigma overshadowed her stature at the time.

However, even by 8th grade, she was starting to suspect something strange was going on. She'd been held back a year, mostly due to her relocation before the orphanage. She was 15, but about the size of a 4th grader. Her teachers didn't care since she had no problems with the class work. Her classmates didn't care since they'd known her all the way through school. Her caretakers didn't care because she wasn't actively dying. They were hilariously overworked and barely had time to pay her or the other children any attention.

The next year, when she went to high school, she just let everyone assume she was 15, not 16. That gained her one year, but she stayed scrawny and flat-chested anyway, with a body of an eleven-year-old. None of her friends really seemed to mind. She assumed that they just whispered about her behind her back. Maybe they blamed it on an imaginary mother who smoked too much or on some kind of terribly deficient nutritional situation at the orphanage. If they had their suspicions, they never brought them up to her, and neither was there any mention of it from her teachers. Hani didn't bring it up either. She knew it must be related to her time before the orphanage and she didn't need anyone thinking she was crazy or a liar on top of being some kind of neglected malnourished elf-girl too.

High school continued to pass as normally as could have been expected. One benefit from her slow body development was that she didn't start getting hit with hormones until senior year. Everyone else seemed to go partially crazy. They worried about so many inconsequential things, were radically distracted by their attractions and infatuations, and generally annoyed Hani. But it wasn't much of a blessing since her development just got delayed instead.

Senior year got weird. Acne started and didn't go away for several years. She began to understand the interest in boys, but they almost entirely ignored her. It was isolating, but it wasn't a surprise, and it was something she was well accustomed to. The orphanage wasn't a warm place to grow up.

One day really stood out at the end of high school. Hani had come home from school and was greeted with a letter in her cubby. This was extremely unusual since she didn't correspond with anyone outside the city. She pulled out the letter and saw the return address to Oberlin ... the only college she had applied to. Oberlin had impressed her when she'd examined the history of their ground-breaking policy of allowing women to attend when other colleges didn't. It didn't hurt that their educational track record was amazing too. Her grades were decent, but she knew she was facing some serious competition.

She had ripped open the letter. With hands shaking, she'd extracted the paper from the envelope and started reading. She scanned past the return address, her address, and the salutation. The body of the letter started with "Congratulations." She felt the tears of relief welling up as she'd skimmed the rest of the letter. Most of it was mechanical details about what she needed to do next, the dates of various milestones, and the like. While she would soon be out of the orphanage regardless, now she had a chance at a serious education.

Hani smiled to herself about the memory and continued to mind the darkening highway. She still had that letter, too. It was in the back seat, in fact, with all her other crucial belongings. She flipped on her headlights and checked her watch. At least another hour to North Platte; she was very close to being able to sleep in her new home.

As she came over a small rise, she noticed a delivery truck in the oncoming lanes slowly crossing from the slow lane into the passing lane. It wasn't signaling and it didn't have its headlights on. Hani frowned and studied the truck. Without any warning, it veered into the grass highway divider and came barreling toward her. She slammed on her brakes and tried to dodge away, but the truck kept turning in a giant arc toward her car. The driver must have either fallen asleep or died and had just cranked the wheel further and further to the left as it came tearing across the highway.

The angled front tire of the truck hit the edge of the pavement and must have caught slightly. The forward momentum of the truck got partially converted into rotation and the truck started to flip. Even after all this, and Hani's heavily applied brakes, the vehicles still collided. Or so Hani assumed since she had stopped being in her car. The world had shifted to the gray she'd only seen a few times before and the vehicles flashed through and behind her. The world snapped back to full color and she felt herself tumbling through the air.

Well away from the highway now, Hani tore through a low bush and then slammed into the ground, skidding through grass. She lay prone with her eyes closed. Slowly she counted her limbs, and her fingers, waiting for pain. Opening her eyes, she could see back down the highway from where she'd landed. The delivery truck had crushed the driver's side of her car. Nothing moved.

Every inch of her ached, but nothing felt broken. Her shoulder felt the worst. She'd probably landed on it, but it all happened way too fast. She got up and limped back to the wreckage, trying to see if the driver of the truck was okay. The truck lay on its side, though she couldn't see into the cab since it was pitched up across what was left of the hood of her car. She climbed across the wreckage and got a look through the shattered window of the truck. Inside, she could make out a form slumped over the steering wheel.

"Hello! You okay? Can you hear me?" Hani shouted. She couldn't make it up to the driver's side door and the passenger side was pinned under the truck. The man inside didn't move, but let out a faint grunt. "Hold on! I can't get to you, but I'll try to get us help. Hang in there!"

Hani climbed back down, being careful not to gash herself open on anything. As she stepped onto the pavement, her feet hit a puddle. Her car was leaking fluid and she hoped it was coolant. The radiator was pretty well destroyed. No gasoline, please no gasoline.

Cars coming her direction would be forced to stop, but really unobservant drivers on the other side might just keep going. She needed to get help for this man quickly. She started jogging down the median shoulder of the oncoming lanes, hoping for some more traffic. It wasn't that late and this was a big highway. Yes, it was Nebraska, but they had to have put a highway here for a reason.

Just as she started running out of breath, she saw headlights. Hani waved her arms and stepped slightly into the highway. The car was decelerating, thankfully. It pulled up to her and the driver leaned out, "Are you okay?"

"I need help. I was in an accident and the other driver is stuck in his truck," Hani panted.

Her would-be savior turned to his passenger and said, "Chuck, go with her, I'll drive into town and get the hook and ladder."

Hani hadn't even noticed the passenger. Chuck got out and ran around behind the car, joining Hani. He looked at her for a moment and said, "Are you sure you're not hurt?"

"Nothing's broken," Hani assured him.

"You're bleeding," Chuck helpfully pointed out.

"I know, I know," Hani said, trying to hide her frustration. "We have to get back."

"Jerry, get going, I'll help out here until you're back," Chuck said. He followed Hani back across the highway as Jerry tore away at top speed.

They got back to the wreckage and Chuck took a try at reaching the cab. He was taller and not injured. With his advantages, he was able to get the driver's side door open and step up into the cab from what was left of the front wheel. He spent a few seconds in the cab, but Hani couldn't see what he was doing. When he emerged, he looked upset.

"What is it?" Hani said, fingers interlocked on her head.

"I'm sorry Ma'am, we weren't fast enough. He didn't make it."

2014, October 4th, Saturday

Rob and Hani enjoyed a quiet breakfast. Hani watched a squirrel outside digging up a good spot to hide nuts. They'd finished out the day yesterday by cleaning up the mess from the firebomb they'd created and retired to the house. In addition to the duffels, Rob had stocked the back of the Jeep with food and beer, so they were prepared for some serious slacking. She wondered if she'd be able to bring herself to get on a plane tomorrow night. Her regular life seemed so bland compared to this.

Rob broke the meal-silence first, "So, anything you want to try out today?"

"I've got a few ideas, but one I'd really like to try," Hani said. She'd been pondering it all night, between the lapses in her fitful sleep.

"I'm all ears," Rob said.

"Well, something stood out yesterday that seemed weird to me. The video showed me vanishing before the gasoline lit. I wonder why that happened. Was I anticipating it?" Hani started to explain.

Rob nodded, "Yeah, I was curious about that too. You think you can control it consciously?"

"I don't feel like I'm selecting when to leave, but maybe it's possible to influence it," Hani guessed. She took a sip of coffee.

Rob screwed up his face, thinking. "Seems like it'd be kind of like moving a limb you've never known you could move before. Less thinking 'move' and more actually moving. What's your plan?"

"Well, I'm hoping it might be like breathing. We need air to live and normally our breathing is autonomically controlled. Its pace increases when we've exerted ourselves and reduces once we've recovered. I can choose to breathe quickly, deeply, slowly, whatever. But I can't hold my breath forever, my body will force it back into action to keep me alive. What if this is like that, only it's much more dramatic about the keeping me alive part? So far, I assume I can't stop myself from vanishing when my life would have been endangered, but what if I can go early, or come back late? Or skip over events that pose no danger to me at all?"

Rob's eyebrows were up. He chewed his toast slowly. "If this works, you could skip over arbitrary spans of time at will."

"Yeah. I haven't really figured out a way that it's particularly useful beyond conflict avoidance," Hani grinned.

"Well, let's see what happens. What did you want to start with?" Rob asked, getting up to take their empty plates to the sink.

"I'd like to start with your pistol again. Skipping certainly feels like something, but I want to try to focus on the moment just before," Hani said.

"Okay, I'll go get it." Rob went to his room and came back with ammo and the pistol. He started loading an empty magazine while Hani finished her coffee before making her way to the front door.

Outside, they resumed their earlier positions. The camera had only gotten dirty and knocked around, so they could still record their experiments. Rob prepared to aim and asked, "Stationary, I assume?"

"Yeah," Hani nodded, "I'll have enough to concentrate on. Though, actually, count to ten between shots."

"You got it." Rob fired a round and Hani blinked out and back into existence.

Hani concentrated on her senses. She unfocused her eyes slightly and felt her breathing. The gun fired again and she skipped over the bullet again. Nothing felt different. She tried to anticipate the next bullet. Rob fired and she imagined she could feel a small tickle at the back of her head as she skipped. The bullet came and went, but she couldn't find the sensation. She focused again, waiting for the bullet, and she felt the tickle again. It was almost like a forgotten memory, or something left unfinished. It was more obscure, though. Not like she forgot to turn off the stove or lock the front door when she left. More like a name she couldn't remember. The next bullet came and went and she missed the sensation again.

She focused on the anticipation and the seemingly lost thought danced just outside her reach as she skipped the incoming bullet. She closed her eyes entirely this time and counted down the ten seconds. As the tenth second unfolded, she caught a thread of her elusive thought and pulled.

Rob eased his finger off the trigger without firing. Hani had popped away and hadn't returned. He glanced at the camera. It was still recording. He started to take a step toward Hani's position but she thumped back into the clearing before he'd taken a single step. She opened her eyes and focused on him. He smiled and congratulated her, "Nice work! You got it?"

Hani let out her breath. She didn't realize she'd been holding it. "I ... I think so? What'd you see?"

"Well, you were gone for about 5 seconds and I never fired," Rob said, waving the gun a little.

"Still rolling?"

"And you called *me* anachronistic!" Rob chided. "Yeah, I didn't stop it."

"Okay, let me try again." Hani felt around in her mind, trying to explore the edges of the anticipation, finding the missing thread, and snagged it. She pulled and tried to hold on this time. The world went gray and silent. The trees waved frantically in the wind and Rob shifted his weight from foot to foot rapidly before suddenly sitting down. Fear started creeping in. What if she got stuck like this? She felt the thread slipping, but she held on to it and started counting to help her focus. The clouds shot past, and the sun swung overhead. She got to "three" and let go.

Rob's head snapped up from his seat on the ground. "Well that seemed to work!"

Hani held her head and let out her breath, "Shit, that's hard. I feel like I just took like 20 standardized tests."

"I was worried we'd broken you! The camera battery ran out a couple hours ago, but I didn't want to get the extension cord to charge it, in case I missed anything. You held that for over three hours!" Rob got up and offered her a hand.

Hani took his hand and stepped forward. She was shaky, like she was coming down from an adrenaline rush. They left the clearing and sat on the porch steps. Hani was surprised it worked so easily. She'd just never had the opportunity to really study the ability. And to think, she could have skipped so many boring days with this.

"You hungry, thirsty, tired?" Rob offered.

"Not really. I'd mentioned it before, but time doesn't pass the same while I'm skipping. I counted to three once I realized I'd triggered it. You said I was gone for three hours?" Hani double-checked.

"Yeah. If you want to try again, I could prop the kitchen clock up on a chair for you to watch while you're skipping," Rob suggested.

"Yeah!" Hani didn't feel tired at all. She followed Rob inside. He pointed out the clock and picked up a chair. Hani plucked the clock off the wall and they returned to the clearing outside. Rob set the chair down and then headed back to the house. Hani situated the clock on the chair to her satisfaction and waited for Rob to return. The front door squeaked as Rob came back outside with a second chair. He positioned it next to the first one and sat down in it.

"The ground is a little wet," he explained.

Hani chuckled and took a few steps back. "You ready?"

"Me? You're the one bending time! Go for it," Rob said.

Hani stared at the clock and sneaked up on the thread she'd only just found. She missed it a few times, and then calmed her mind for a second, trying to surprise it. She took hold and the clock's minute hand started spinning rapidly. She counted it out to herself. "One, one thousand. Two, one thousand."

Rob did something rapidly with his hands and face that she couldn't make out.

"Three, one thousand. Four, one thousand." Coming at this calmly made it easier to hang on to. There wasn't as much of a sense of anticipation or dread. And the fear was gone since she knew how to stop. "Five, one thousand."

It was starting to get dark. She let go.

Rob smiled at her from his seat. "I'm glad I got a snack when I brought out my chair!"

"Ah! That's what you were doing. I couldn't see what was going on with your face."

"So, you could see the clock?" Rob asked.

"Yeah, the minute hand tore through the hours. To me, the

clock's hour hand seemed to move just a little bit faster than my counting of seconds. It didn't look like it was exactly one second for every hour. It looked like just a few minutes more than a full hour per second I counted," Hani detailed.

Rob nodded. "Is it variable at all?"

"It didn't seem that way. I was much calmer this time, and the sun seemed to move at about the same speed," Hani said.

"Well, I'm famished. You want dinner?" Rob asked.

"Well, actually, no. For me, it's still a bit after breakfast," Hani said, considering her full stomach.

"Heh, this is going to mess up your sleep schedule," Rob pointed out.

"Yeah, but I can also just skip tonight while you sleep. I can join you after breakfast," Hani said with a grin. "What a great way to solve jet lag!"

Rob laughed, stood up, and cleared the clock off the chair, offering her the seat. Hani thanked him and sat down.

"Is this okay? Waiting around for me wasn't boring for you?" Hani asked.

Rob laughed again. "No way. This is great. Let me tell you about boring …"

1761

Since Pierre had moved from London to Paris, things hadn't gone as well as he'd hoped. Half the money he'd saved had gotten stolen and the other half had gone into setting up an estate on the edge of the city. It looked like the farm would stay self-sustaining. He'd be able to pay the farmers and the servants, but there wasn't much left for himself. He was barely able to keep food on the table for all of them.

He departed the estate, leaving his Paris lawyer in charge of keeping things running, and spent time looking for a job he might be able to build from the ground up. Besides his obvious advantage in the area of never dying, he was fluent in more languages than most of the traders that visited port. He hoped demonstrating only the latter ability would be sufficient.

He spent time visiting various shipping companies and finally found an opening with a Portuguese company that was doing a lot of sailing to the New World. They had a large stake in a West Indies coffee settlement and they made the rounds through Europe and back, hauling supplies and people in one direction and coffee in the other.

They needed someone to facilitate a new settlement expansion and they were spread too thin. He impressed them with his French, English, German, Italian, Spanish, and Portuguese. His Dutch and Danish were a little rusty, but workable. Between his languages, his societal position, and his willingness to leave immediately, he was a very desirable find as far as they were concerned.

Pierre figured he could move up the ranks and either build the settlement into something he had partial ownership in, or at least he'd gain the operational knowledge to set up his own. The promised bonuses looked like he'd have enough saved after a few decades to build up the Paris estate the way he wanted.

He wondered briefly what things would have been like if he'd just stayed in London. The estate there had gotten quite large, but he was too well known. Selling it and relocating seemed like the only way to maintain his cover and retain some of the wealth he'd built up, but that meant he couldn't continue to grow it. The trading company angle seemed like a good way to go. If he could build the company and stay at an arm's length from it, things would be much easier to move around. Estates didn't really offer that kind of malleability. Everyone knew you and there wasn't much of a way to escape it.

He continued to hope that some day he'd at least be able to collect the journals he'd left behind. He was fairly certain no one was going to be able to translate them. At least not anyone in London. They'd have to reach much further to find someone who could read Arabic.

Growing "old" in a community hadn't worked well before, so avoiding that was now the first rule. He wanted to explore the world more, but that required a fair bit of money to do without a lot of suffering. Staying out of prison or slavery was tricky if you weren't part of a given culture or didn't have the money to keep the local authorities happy. Not dying doesn't really help if you're chained up.

He was set to start his adventures the very next day, so he packed up clothes, money, and a few things he held dear. One item was a pocket watch given to him by a friend about a hundred years earlier. Pierre had saved his friend's family from a building fire. The Black Death consumed his friend only a little while later. He'd stayed in contact with the family for a few decades more, by letter courier, but once the children had grown and had their own families, Pierre had let them go. The watch reminded him of them.

With his affairs in a hopefully stable arrangement, he boarded the *Fogo Eterno*. He was pleased with the ship. Her name felt appropriate for his condition. The crew was as polite as he might expect, but when he put his back into helping with chores they became downright friendly. He didn't mind work and preferred their rowdy company to just sitting in his cabin staring at the ocean. Rowdy was perfect for him.

After about four weeks of helping with rigging, cleaning, food preparation, and anything else that anyone felt like teaching him, he was really enjoying the voyage. The rum was amazing, but they tried to keep it to a minimum lest crew start slipping overboard. The seas were getting rougher.

Pierre woke up one particular evening when the ship pitched him from his cot. He landed hard on the deck and tried to stand. A crash of thunder outside cleared his mind, while the snap of lightning that accompanied it flared through the gaps around his cabin door. The floor twisted out from under him while he tried to claw his way to the door. He unlatched it and it burst inwards, salt water washing through the room. The *Fogo Eterno* tilted back and the floating contents of his cabin tried to escape out the door, tossing him forward on to the main deck. The crew were barely hanging on from various ropes, railings, and gratings.

Lightning ripped through the sky again and Pierre could see the rear mast was gone. The captain was spinning the wheel, desperately trying to line himself up with the swells. The other two sails were mostly stowed and he could almost make out some of the shouting. His friend with the rum slid past and grabbed him with both hands, shouting, "This is the end! Netuno has come for us!"

The ship rode the side of a wave. The swell thrust them down onto the deck. Pierre clawed at the planking, trying to find a grip. The wave crested and the *Fogo Eterno* started to float for a moment. The wave receded and she rolled to her side. Crew fell into the sea and Pierre joined them, screaming as he waved his hands trying to catch a rope that lashed past him. The sea swallowed him and he heard nothing but water pressing against him. Lightning flashed, casting shadows of the ship and her floating crew.

Pierre tried to figure out which way was up and seemed to constantly fail at it. He could feel the surging of the waves as he was pressed and pulled. His air ran out and he started drowning. His lungs lit on fire as the salt water was forced in. He started to black out, only to have the sights and sounds surge back into his consciousness. He choked and thrashed, trying to escape the water's grip. It was not ready to let him go and he died again.

He came to. The water was stabbing him in the lungs again. His eyes went from numb to burning and back again. He was not dead, but he was not living. He tried to control his panic and fear, but he kept losing track of his thoughts. The pain was everywhere and nowhere. Each time he thought he might be making progress, he realized he was just dying in the ocean again.

Time had no meaning and thoughts kept escaping his mind. He knew he existed, but he couldn't remember where or how. At some point, he felt his mind coalescing again. He couldn't see, but he realized he was breathing again. And cold. The cold was terrible. He was shivering. He tried moving and realized the storm was gone. The water remained. He opened his eyes and was stung with salt. The sky was turning orange. Turning to the east, he watched the sun come up on a roiling ocean.

He kept losing feeling in his hands and feet; they kept cycling back in and out of numbness. Pierre couldn't figure out what he was going to do. There seemed to be no trace of the ship or her crew. He was closer to America than France at this point in the trip. Stopping death was not the problem. He was going to need to swim for a long time. He watched the sun some more and decided to just start. He went west.

On the evening of the first night, the sharks found him. Drowning was familiar now. Salt was a way of life. Exhaustion was constant. But the sharks were new. He couldn't decide if it was worse than the drowning. He tried to keep them at bay, kicking at them when they swung past his legs. Eventually they took a few bites and then there was nothing he could do. They tore the flesh from his body and he just replaced it. The sting of the salt merged with their horrible teeth was like an endless blender.

Eventually they left him; they couldn't eat any more. He drifted and tried to sleep. It did not come, so he watched the stars like he used to and picked out his favorite constellations. They watched over him, passively recording his suffering.

He swam again the next day. At evening, the sharks returned. There were more of them. He tried to ball up, making himself a smaller target. This was a mistake as they ended up biting him in half. The world stopped and, when he could think again, it felt like he was in a cave that was shrinking. His bones broke as it crushed him. A split second later he understood he had regrown inside a shark. He tried thrashing around as the body of the shark split open.

He emerged and bobbed to the surface, gagging on gore: the shark's and his own. He gasped for air and was pulled down again.

When they left, he floated for a while, trying to figure out if he had any weapons, or any other defense. Nothing came to mind. He wasn't able to sleep, so he gave up on only swimming during the day. The stars could guide him just as well as the sun. Better, in some cases. He wasn't picky.

A week into his cycle of being devoured and swimming, he wondered why he hadn't gone completely mad. He wasn't sleeping, but the mirages he saw never got any worse. He assumed that each time he literally lost his head, it was replaced with a fresh one. If he ever escaped the ocean, he wondered if he might skip sleeping by just chopping off his head every night. Maybe he *was* going mad.

Whales visited a few times. They were curious, but ultimately couldn't help him. They spent time swimming alongside him and eventually they'd dive and vanish from sight. Their company was consoling, if short-lived.

Between the Atlantic currents and his swimming, it took almost a month to reach land. He knew he was getting close when, during the days, he could make out ships in the distance. He tried waving at them, but they never saw him. He would be consumed by sharks once again.

Finally, he washed up on the shore near Caracas. He was naked and cold. The sharks hadn't found him this last evening. He'd been in too shallow water, he assumed. He dragged himself from the sea and lay just out of reach of the ocean's grasp. The stars beamed down at him, still silent to his plight. He rolled over and coughed up water, clearing more salt from his lungs. He lay still on the ground, trying to remember what land felt like.

He slept and dreamed of sharks and lightning. The faces of the crew slewed past him and he could see his pocket watch drifting to the ocean floor.

2010, Summer

"Please stay, Jonesy," Crawford begged.

Jonesy picked up her purse and looked at the floor. "I ... I can't any more, Professor. I've been volunteering here for a year now, and you were barely able to pay me before that. I'm still in school and I'm months behind on my rent." She looked up at him and met his eyes. "This work is important, but I can't do it any more. I can't throw my life away any more."

Crawford's shoulders slumped. He looked around his workshop and nodded slowly. She was the last to go. Again. He'd run out of money twice since founding Tillinghast Research. Most of the staff he'd acquired had left during the first funding interruption. A few stayed and made it until Crawford had discovered another small group of investors, but their money had run out almost a year ago. Jonesy had been the only one to continue to spend time working with him.

The two of them had been to countless venture capitalists, but now the field had totally dried up. The sub-prime mortgage collapse in 2008 had everyone holding their purse strings very tightly. Even with the little portable rig they used for demonstrations, no one wanted to take a risk on his creation. He was starting to suspect that the venture capitalists were talking behind his back. It might have even been fueled by his dispute with the University. The Board of Regents were spreading lies about his research's viability.

"Please consider talking to the Navy," Jonesy said. "I know you vowed not to deal with the government, but they have the money."

"No."

"Then come back to the University, teach the—"

"No."

Jonesy gathered herself, and tried one last time. "Your house is gone. Your wife isn't speaking to you. The lease is up on this place next week, and I don't remember the last time I saw you eat."

Crawford glared at her.

Jonesy sighed, looked away, and walked to the door. She paused with her hand on the doorknob and turned to look back at Crawford. He had closed his eyes and was clenching his fists at his side. "Just talk to them." She opened the door. "They might be able to get you what you need."

"No!" Crawford shrieked and clapped his hands to his ears. When he opened his eyes again, Jonesy was gone.

* * *

Crawford sat, waiting, in the hallway on a wooden bench. He hated Arlington, but he tried to put it out of his mind. He'd justified this trip by trying to imagine that maybe the government would pay back the world for his son's death. If he could really secure serious funding from them, maybe the world could finally be made a better place.

His stomach growled. He'd used his last few dollars getting his suit cleaned. Thankfully, Jonesy had lent him her transit card for the Metro. He hoped he wasn't sweating too much from the walk from the train station. The two Pelican Cases weren't heavy, but they were bulky. Without someone helping him roll them around, it was rather awkward navigating elevators, much less escalators.

The doors next to the bench opened and a man with a crew-cut leaned out, first looking up the hallway toward empty benches, then back down toward Crawford. "Ah, Mr Tillinghast, they're ready for you now."

"Doctor," Crawford corrected.

"Doctor! Yes, sorry," the man nodded. "Can I help with that?" he offered, stepping out into the hallway.

Crawford gratefully let him roll one of the cases into the meeting room. Crawford followed, nodded briefly to the people gathered at the large oval table, and started to unpack his cases onto the center of the table.

"Good afternoon," one of them said, but Crawford wasn't looking at them. He'd seen their uniforms when he walked through the door. Six of them, not including the soldier currently walking back toward the hallway to shut the doors. He could feel his stomach turning, but he fought to treat this like any other venture capitalist meeting.

Jonesy had done an amazing job designing their portable demonstration rig. The batteries and power regulator fit into one case and the resonance focusing system fit in the other. It only took him a few minutes to get the optics and power-couples attached. He could feel the group of people studying him. "Just one more moment," he said quietly.

"Tillinghast, I'm Lieutenant Commander Samuels. Thank you for joining us today. I read your proposal. It's very bold, and I only understood pieces of it. I brought in a few of my specialists," Samuels nodded to a woman and two men on his left. "They were intrigued.

My counterparts in the Army, though, were less impressed," Samuels nodded to two bored looking men on his right.

Crawford straightened up after double-checking the batteries and flipped on the power system. It hummed comfortingly. He closed his eyes, took a deep breath, and opened them again. He put on a smile. "Hello! Thank you for seeing me. I'd like to show you the future of energy production. Did you bring your own measurement tools, like I mentioned on the phone?"

Samuels turned to his people, "Landon?"

Landon jumped up, and brought over some gear. "Doctor," he nodded. "Connect here for load and voltage, yes?" he said, holding out measurement leads.

"Yes," Crawford answered, attaching Landon's gear to the resonance rig. "This is our resonance and phase regulation equipment, and this is the reaction area. You can measure what I'm putting into the system here, and you can measure what is being produced on this side. As described, this system generates almost more energy than we put in." He pressed the red button near the edge of the reaction area.

Surrounded by the reaction area's array of lenses, a golf-ball sized sphere sparked to life above the reaction area, glowing evenly. Crawford listened to the steady throb of the orb. He thought it sounded hungry.

Landon studied his equipment, frowning slightly.

"It isn't much, but you can see the output is non-linear. As we put more energy in, we get exponentially more energy out." Crawford slowly turned a knob next to the red button, and the sphere sagged slightly and turned darker. Patterns played across its surface. They were beautiful.

The two Army representatives suddenly perked up, glancing at each other.

Landon nodded slowly. "It's still not producing anywhere near enough to be self-sustaining, but the output did jump. If the math you proposed holds, it wouldn't take much power to get this initiated."

Crawford nodded. "This is where my research is heading. The best we did was 90% containment, but it turns out the challenge here is more about regulation and resonance control than just raw power. I'm proposing that a new resonance control system be built which can handle the phase shifts we've measured. From there, we can continue to raise the power levels."

Samuels looked around the table. Landon shrugged his shoulders slightly and nodded slowly. The two Army representatives were talking quietly with each other, brows furrowed. Samuels asked simply, "How much do you need?"

"Tillinghast, wait," one of Army representatives spoke up finally. "Have you done any spectroscopic analysis of the ... reaction area?"

"Doctor," Crawford tried to correct them again.

"What?"

Crawford sighed. "Yes, of course," he answered impatiently, "You can find them near the end of the proposal."

The Army representatives shuffled their papers. Landon produced his copy, flipped it to the analysis, and handed it over. They read it in silence, bent over the same page.

Crawford's attention was split between watching them, watching the orb, and wondering if there was going to be lunch.

"Did you solve the phase stabilization?"

"I built an adaptive system that can keep ahead of the shifts," Crawford answered quickly.

The two looked at the orb, then studied Crawford. Finally, one turned to Samuels and said, "We need to get this equipment to our facility as soon as possible. Tillinghast has a project to run."

2014, October 5th, Sunday

Rob emerged from his bedroom, stretching his arms over his head and yawning. He enjoyed sleeping. He had his nightmares from time to time, but some nights Marie visited him. Some nights he was roasting a boar with a neighbor. Sleep was peaceful for him and he had come around the other side of hating to wake up. A long time ago, mornings were a reminder of his condition. Now, though, he was beginning to sense his purpose. Or at least, he felt it was right to explore every day. At the worst, he was a witness to the world, no matter how small.

He rifled through the cabin's small fridge, collecting breakfast. He started the coffee and glanced at the clock propped up on the kitchen table. He'd slept in. He crossed the room, keeping out of the center of the room like he was avoiding a grave. He took a seat with his back to the windows, facing into the kitchen. The meal was simple and small, just cold left-overs from yesterday's lunch plans that they never dug into. He finished his meal and sat, patiently waiting.

With a puff of air and almost inaudibly deep thump, Hani resumed her place in the regular stream of time at the center of the kitchen.

"You missed breakfast," Rob said, knowing full well that was the point.

"Ha ha," Hani mocked. "I just had breakfast like an hour ago."

"You still feeling okay? No sudden headaches? Nose bleeds? Langoliers? I have no idea what the stresses or side-effects of this could be," Rob wondered.

"Nothing I can feel, no. I've been through much longer ... but I had no idea what was happening that time. I thought I was dead." Hani tried to push it out of her mind.

"Fair enough. What do you want to do now?" Rob asked, setting his plate in the sink.

"Well, I don't want to live a normal life any more. I've spent almost 70 years just kind of ignoring what I could do. This thing is unlike anything anyone's ever seen ... excepting you. I can't keep going to work every day thinking I'm just a little strange." Hani had been exploring this idea only a short time, but it felt right.

Rob looked nervous. "What did you have in mind?"

"First, is this interesting to you? Do you find this as thrilling as I do?" Hani asked, her eyes searching his.

"I do." Rob looked satisfied. "I really do. I know I'm a bit flat, but this isn't like anything I've been through before. It means we're not alone. There might be more like us. Are we all different?"

"Exactly! So ... this is a bit forward, but I saw your place in the Pearl. And this place here. You've got money, clearly. I don't know from where, but could you provide me with room and board? I'd like to keep exploring this. I could, I don't know, be your accountant? Clean?" Hani had arrived at the edge of her plan. It wasn't much more than just trying to find the limits of her powers.

Rob put up an eyebrow. "Done. Only I've already got an accountant and a cleaner. How about you be my Fellow? I can be a Patron of the Arts, only the art in question is us trying to figure you out."

"Deal!" Hani almost shouted. Was giddiness a side effect of her skipping? Probably not.

She had to make some arrangements. There wasn't really any work for her left to clean up back at the office. She'd cleared her desk of cases in preparation for her no-longer-a-wild-goose-chase vacation time. Her lease was up on February 1st, so she'd have to handle that. She had plenty of savings to cover the three months. She could fly back at some point before February and pack up her stuff.

"Hmm," Rob mused. "Either we'll need a new base of operations, or I need to clear out my office at home to get the second bedroom back in service."

"Totally up to you. I need to send some emails. I've got a job to quit." Hani fetched her laptop. She'd never quit a job before. She always moved offices instead. Drafting a letter of resignation was not going to be particularly fun. She paused for a moment and looked up at Rob. "Actually, is there anything you've had trouble with at the Social Security Office? Anything I can clean up before I'm out of there?"

Rob pondered for a bit, considering options. "Actually, I think I'm okay. Traditionally, I've taken a very slow approach to building new identities. I've gotten extremely good at cycling money through people that don't exist and building a paper trail. It became clear back in the 1920s it was going to be important. I could see that the United States was starting to really track people and money.

"What I've started looking at now is expanding to other countries. Canada was pretty easy to get established in, and I've been working on a few European contingencies too. My relocation plan from the East Coast to the West Coast was seriously botched, though. I think I've solved the problems I created for myself there. I got stupid, but I think I learned a lot." Rob said.

"Well, I'm glad you got stupid," Hani reminded him. "We'd never have met."

"Yup, good point." Rob confirmed. He considered their new arrangement for a moment, then said, "Are you sure you want this? You're leaving behind a job you seem to have been really attached to for a long time."

"Yeah, I'm sure. I never really belonged there. I kept people at an arm's length most of the time so they wouldn't notice how slowly I aged. The job was comforting, though. It was like an extension of the orphanage, only being there was my choice. And it was only from 9 to 5. The rest of the day was my own. So with both comfort and freedom, it was certainly appealing. But I don't want to go back to that. I can't go back to that. I really need to figure out why I've got this ability. And probably more importantly, what I should be doing with it," Hani explained.

"You familiar with Spider-Man?" Rob asked. "I read a few when they were first published, but lost interest until the movies started coming out a few years back."

"Yeah, sure. I bet I know what you're going to say," Hani grinned.

"Well, it's a solid quote. 'With great power comes great responsibility,'" Rob repeated.

"Completely true. You've obviously had time to think about this. Why are you hiding out in a condo? Your efforts during World War I couldn't have gone unrecognized. Why not become a super hero or a vigilante?"

1587

The war in Cologne was winding down and Karl was glad he'd managed to entirely avoid it. He'd moved to Olevia, a village outside of Verdun, within the Electorate of Trier. It was a simple farming community and he was glad to find work as a plowman. It was not easy work, but it paid well enough. He had a room and three meals a day. No one asked him any questions.

It had been almost seven years since he'd settled here. He knew most of the town. It was a pretty tight-knit village. The weekends were spent in the pub, with a pause for Sunday prayers. The farmers knew how to relax. During the week, it was a return to the back-breaking slog of the fields. Karl didn't get as tired as the others and it didn't go unnoticed. When someone had an especially hard section of field to work, they would tend to ask Karl for a favor. He was happy to help out. It wasn't much different from the general village-wide barn-raising sense of community everyone held.

He rented his room from a married couple, Olga and Franz, who had been very generous to him when he'd first arrived in the village. Olga worked as a baker at the Sword and Shield Inn near the edge of town. She was helping wait tables when Karl had first arrived. He'd asked around for more permanent lodging beyond just the Inn and she'd said to talk to Franz on Sunday. He stuck around, went to church, and chatted with Franz about staying in their spare room. It worked very well for everyone and Karl hadn't ever considered moving since that day.

The village of Olevia wasn't rich, although they did well for themselves. They weren't particularly cosmopolitan and they weren't near any big trading routes. They had reasonable proximity to Verdun, and anyone growing up in Olevia who wanted to see The City tended to move there. Olevia unintentionally stayed in the shadows, but few of the residents minded their lack of notoriety.

The war had really drained resources throughout the Electorates and the tax collectors had been getting more and more demanding. Olevia finally caught their attention and they started hiking tax rates. For a few years, this just caused some grumbling. But since the area stayed safe and people's quality of life was relatively unchanged, it just stayed grumbling. Later in the war, though, it became a problem and disputes started to crop up.

One farmer, Frederick, and his family had just lost a lot of supplies and equipment in a fire, but the tax collectors still demanded their full cut. Fredrick couldn't afford to pay the taxes if his family were going to continue working the land. They tried to negotiate with the collectors and, with many other families offering their support and equipment, they almost made ends meet. This delayed things for a while, but ultimately the collectors returned. Stories differ about what happened, but Karl boiled the essentials down to the final results. When the collectors left, they took one of Fredrick's daughters and Frederick gained a broken leg.

The village was incensed, but they had no recourse. As the weeks continued, the collectors returned. Emboldened by their successful terrorizing of Fredrick's family, they started taking more and more from the village. When they arrived at Franz's farm and demanded their payments, Karl went out to the barn and picked out one of the recently sharpened hoes. When he returned, Franz was in a heated debate with one of the collectors.

There were eight of them. Six were clearly there as Muscle, armed with swords and light armor. Karl wondered what kind of man would join the tax collectors to harass farmers. Karl eyed them and listened to the argument as it escalated. As he closed the distance between himself and Franz, the Muscle noticed and started drawing swords. The second collector demanded Olga go with them until Franz was able to pay. Franz laughed at him and spat in his face.

"There's no more discussion to be had here," the collector said, slowly wiping his face of Franz's collected saliva. "We're going to take her, take anything of value here, and burn the house to the ground. Now either you two can help us, or you can get in the way. I don't recommend getting in the way."

Karl eyed the closest of the Muscle. "Franz, can you step back into the house? I need to have a quick chat with these nice men."

Franz stared at Karl, looking confused. He couldn't understand that Karl was intent on a fight.

Karl repeated, "Franz. Step into the house. Now."

Franz started to object, "What do you—"

Karl spun completely around while hefting the hoe from his shoulder. It gained significant momentum as it came around and got buried in the nearest Muscle's hip, who bellowed in agony and crumpled to the ground. Karl had pulled himself forward after impact and caught the man's sword before it touched the ground. He launched himself across the fallen Muscle and speared the next through the throat before he'd even been able to turn. The man gurgled in surprise and grabbed for his own neck, trying to hold in the river of blood.

The remaining four Muscle had enough time to react and had

taken up defensive positions between Karl and the house. Franz had backed away, in surprise initially, but after seeing the second Muscle drop, he'd thrown himself inside the house. The second collector had lunged after him, but got a door to the face as Franz slammed it shut.

Karl parried several strikes, but was dramatically outnumbered. A sword slashed at his free arm and it bled briefly. He winced and ignored it. They had expected him to slow, and he used it to his advantage, disarming a third while tripping him to the ground. A fourth stabbed him in the gut and tried to get the sword all the way through him. Karl felt it ripping through organs and tried to tune out the agony. With his free hand he grabbed his attacker by the pauldron and drew his blade across the man's neck.

The tripped Muscle got back up, looking for his sword, while the other two stepped back, waiting for Karl to fall from his injury. Karl let his limp attacker drop back from him. The sword that had been impaled in his stomach slid out, dragged away by the grip his attacker's body retained. He pivoted and swung, winding up speed on his sword. He connected with the knee of the man who was bent over collecting his dropped sword. The Muscle went down again, crying out.

The two unarmed tax collectors were busy banging on the door of the house, seemingly unaware of the trouble their Muscle was having with the lone farmer. Karl stared at the two remaining combatants. They looked slightly confused, but mostly angry and impatient. Deciding the gut wound wasn't as bad as it had seemed, they resumed their attack. Karl parried one, and the other connected across his chest, cutting a trough and knocking him off balance.

Karl stumbled to his knees and free hand, managing to keep his sword up, deflecting another blow. As he tried to roll away to stand, one of his attackers landed a strike to his head, cleaving his skull deeply. Karl lost control of his body and twitched onto his side. His vision had blanked out, but it returned with a flare. He collected his sword and stood up. His attackers now looked more confused than angry.

Karl ran at one of them and traded attacks and blocks for a few seconds. Karl felt another sword stab him through the back, breaking several ribs in the process. He cried out, spraying the other with blood. His lung must have been punctured too. The man in front of him paused his assault briefly and Karl swung at his ankle, crushing the bones here. The Muscle dropped like a brick as Karl felt the sword in his back dislodge.

As he turned, he caught the tip of a sword across his face, neck, and shoulder. Bits of flesh dropped to the ground as Karl snarled at the last standing assailant. The man stepped back several feet, now looking terrified. The confusion had been handily replaced by fear. Karl lunged at him and chopped at the man's head. The Muscle's arms were raised trying to block the attack, but Karl eventually got through the armor with his repeated blows. The man was yelling, begging for his life, as he fell back, tripping on his own feet. Karl ignored his cries and impaled him in the face.

The last armed man was crawling away toward the house. The two tax collectors had given up their fist assault on the house at some point and gaped at the supposed farmer awash in blood, shirt shredded, standing with their hired swordsmen fanned out on the ground around him. Karl walked over to the man with ankle problems, and relieved him of his head.

"Never come back to this town," Karl snarled at the collectors. They both fled, giving Karl a wide birth. They mounted their horses and galloped away. Karl dropped his borrowed sword and gathered the six horses the fallen Muscle had left behind.

Franz emerged from the house, followed by Olga.

"I think we need to burn these bodies," Karl suggested.

Franz continued to silently survey the carnage.

Unfazed, Olga nodded and said, "I will get wood."

Franz studied Karl for a few moments. "You have damned us all." Franz took one of the horses and rode away toward the center of the village. Karl slumped his shoulders and sat on the ground, catching his breath.

By the time Franz had returned with several other villagers, Olga and Karl had built a large pile of wood and kindling, enough to hold all the bodies. Olga stepped away from the pile and joined her husband. Franz dismounted and pointed at Karl.

The other men dismounted and surrounded Karl. One had rope. Karl cried out as they grabbed at him, restraining him. "Franz! What's going on? I just saved your family from certain death."

"I will have no witch in my house, nor in my village. You are spawn of the fallen. I have seen it with my own eyes," Franz replied. His face was strained.

"Witches must burn." Olga said plainly.

"Olga!" Karl yelled, "You've been my host for years! I've done no harm!"

One of the men holding him slashed his shoulder with a knife. It healed instantly. The others murmured in surprise and anger. Karl made out "Unnatural," "Satan's work," and "Burn him!" They bound him tightly and lashed him to one of the logs he'd dragged out in front of the house with Olga. Karl's disappointment was now colliding with his anger and anticipation of pain.

They lit the fire and stood back. Franz and Olga looked disgusted. The others appeared scared but resolute. Karl tried to prepare himself for the fire. As it reached him, his clothes and hair started burning. His skin seared and healed, like a flag thrashing in the wind, back and forth between two directions. As the heat intensified, he just healed faster. His vision flickered in and out as his eyes fluctuated through various states of repair. The pain was staggering but punctuated with areas of numbness. He tried to not scream, but there wasn't much reason to hold it in.

The villagers looked even more terrified as they watched Karl resist the fire. One intrepid soul fetched a sword from the collected pile Olga and Karl had made not an hour earlier. The villager chopped at Karl's neck. His neck healed quickly, but the man eventually got ahead of it and severed Karl's head from his body. Karl's mind emerged from unbeing and had its senses assaulted by the fire again. The man was shouting in alarm, running from the flaming head that had rolled from Karl's body, only to be replaced anew.

The ropes burned through a few moments later and Karl clambered from the pyre. The flames licked at him for a few more seconds before they extinguished. The villagers drew back, uncertain what to do about this monstrosity. Karl walked, unhindered, to the pile of dead mercenaries. He worked to remove some clothes, armor, and equipment from one that was about his size. He ignored the religious chanting from behind him and got dressed. Another life of his had ended. How far would he have to ride to escape this?

When he went to pick out a horse, half the villagers had scattered. The remaining continued to chant and damn him. They kept their distance, though. Karl didn't say a word and hefted himself up into his horse's saddle.

1948, January

The Emerson School for Children in Massachusetts had been Hani's home for almost three years now. The children were nice to her and the staff were relatively attentive. Hani wished her parents would come get her, but the reality of her situation was finally sinking in. The disappointment over Santa Claus was still fresh, so she continued to hold on to the hope that her parents would come get her.

She was convinced that they would be able to find her in America. The staff had assured her. She tried not to think about their similar claims about Santa Claus. But even if it wasn't Santa delivering the presents, she was still getting presents. She understood the staff was responsible and they'd talked to her about keeping the tradition alive for the other children. She just wished her parents would come get her. She'd trade that for all presents forever.

They'd told her that she and her parents were from Germany, but that she was in the United States now. She remembered the plane ride. It was like the longest car ride she'd ever been on and way more bumpy. There was a tiny toilet. It felt just big enough for her. She couldn't understand how any of the Army men could possibly fit in that little room. She didn't want to think about the Army men. It reminded her too quickly of the circumstances that led up to first meeting them.

After she came to the orphanage, learning English had been

quick. She still struggled with some words. The other children giggled at her strange phrasing, but she couldn't help it. Several of the staff spoke German with her, but even they didn't understand the couple of Yiddish phrases she knew.

She'd started second grade this year. It had been pretty uneventful, but she liked the subjects. They spent a lot more time inside now that it was so cold. She missed running around between the trees and playing catch with the other girls. She and her friend Judith had gotten in trouble the previous week because they had tried playing catch inside. The window they broke had to be fixed quickly to keep the weather out of their room.

The snow was beautiful here and she caught herself staring out the windows, watching it sprinkle down through the trees outside, instead of paying attention to classes. In Sister Martha's class that was okay, since she was rarely called on. As far as she knew, she was the only German child at the orphanage. She suspected Sister Martha did not like her and tried to ignore that she was in the class.

In Sister Anna's class, though, she was called on constantly. She suspected Sister Anna also did not like her, but expressed it differently. The material wasn't very hard. They'd held her back, but she had caught up quickly with English. It had the same letters. Some of the words were even the same.

The orphanage had a small family of cats. Many of the girls had taken up various chores surrounding their care. Petting the cats was serious business, but what had really fascinated them was the litter of kittens that had arrived a few months earlier. The older girls had built a small box for the mama cat. Hani had wanted to help, but they didn't want to share.

The kittens were so tiny when they first arrived. But now they were bigger and went everywhere around the house. She'd find them in class rooms, in bedrooms, getting kicked out of the kitchen, and sneaking around the halls. Before it snowed, they spent a lot of time outside, like her. She liked the snow a lot more than they did, though. Cold could be solved with more layers. The kittens didn't have that option.

She woke up on a Monday to the sound of mewling. She couldn't figure out where it was coming from and woke Judith up to help her find the kitten. Judith realized it was coming from their recently replaced bedroom window. They lived on the top floor, with only the attic above them. Their window looked out on the slanted roof that covered the lower floors. Judith opened the window and exclaimed at the sight of one of the kittens stuck on the roof, between their window and the window of the room next door.

The sound of their combined yelling roused one of the Sisters, as well as the other children on their floor. Their neighbors opened their window too, trying to coax the kitten back inside. The roof was icy with a thin layer of snow, making it especially slick, so each time the cat tried to take a step, it would slide slightly, and then scramble back to its position between the windows, just out of arm's reach.

The Sister had gone to the neighbor's room since the cat was closer to that window. That room was getting crowded, so Hani returned to her own. Judith was still hanging out their window, trying to encourage the cat to move toward the other room, but it refused to budge. The room was getting increasingly cold, and Hani could only think about how frozen the kitten must be.

She'd left her slippers in the common room last night by the fire, so she slipped on Judith's slippers and asked Judith to move, "I've got a better idea."

Judith turned to look back to the room and frowned. "What?"

"I'm going to just climb out there and fetch him," Hani explained.

"You'll slide off the roof!" Judith exclaimed.

"No I won't. I'll hang on. I can reach him, trust me." Hani said.

Judith shrugged and stepped back. Hani climbed up and stepped through the window, holding the sill tightly with one hand. She carefully stepped around, putting herself between the down slope of the roof and the kitten, who was now plaintively meowing at her.

The Sister who was leaning out of the other window yelled at Hani, "Hanielle! Get back in your room this instant!"

Hani ignored her and stepped up toward the cat, scooping him into her free hand. The cat latched on to her pajamas, never stopping his meowing for a moment. He was very loud. Hani shuffled her feet back toward her window, still holding the edge of the sill for balance. She didn't have the leverage to step back into the window without both hands, so she peeled the cat off her and passed him in to Judith's outstretched hands. With the cat safely back in the room, Hani shifted her weight to one foot to step back in when she lost traction and her feet slipped out from under her.

Hani tried to reach out to the sill with her free hand, but missed and slapped the icy roof instead. Judith cried out in alarm and tried to free herself from the kitten so she could reach Hani, but wasn't fast enough. Hani's remaining grip on the sill failed. She twisted, rolling over on to her back and gravity accelerated her down the slope of the roof. She could see the edge of the roof approaching while she tried to dig her heels into the ice. She scratched at the roof, getting only handfuls of snow, and suddenly the world went gray and silent.

Hani wanted to scream. She was back in Hell and she couldn't move. She could partially shift her perspective around, but not more than a few degrees. The world had lost color while she'd been fixated on the edge of the roof. She could see her legs, but they were faint, just like the first time. She thought her memories of that day had just been a nightmare. She still dreamed of it sometimes. Judith had woken her up from a few of those nightmares, but here it was once more.

Would the Army men save her again? How long would she be here this time? She looked for the sun again and it was visibly moving through the sky, same as before. It was too bright to look at directly, even in this gray world, but she could watch the shadows of the trees slowly sweeping through their day. She could do nothing but wait. One benefit of this state was that she wasn't cold at all. She couldn't feel the prickles of the ice under her fingernails or the wind on her cheeks.

After a few minutes, she noticed her heels had sunken through the roof. Her slippers must have fallen off earlier as she'd slid. It looked like her whole body was sinking through the roof as if the shingles were made of water. As the sun finished its race across the sky, her legs had vanished entirely into the roof. The day went dark and she continued to wait.

Eventually the sun came up again and, as it worked its way toward noon, Hani's sight was starting to become obscured by the roof itself. She'd sunk through it and was looking straight across the ice on the surface. A few minutes later, and she could see only wood grain. There was no light inside the roof, but she could still see its materials. She wondered where the sun was now.

After a little while longer, she could see into the room below the roof. Her body, still in the position it was originally during the slide down the roof, was hovering effortlessly in the air now. Hani figured the top of her head was still in the ceiling. She waited.

A few minutes later and the world snapped back to color and she felt the sickening grip of gravity as she dropped from the ceiling of the bedroom. She bounced off the edge of another child's bed, still traveling forward, and crashed into their dresser, landing with one foot under her. She cried out as something twisted in her ankle and the two children in the room bolted up from their beds.

She lay on the floor, holding her ankle as it slowly swelled. The other girls stared at her for a moment and then one ran out of the room yelling, "Hani's here! We found Hani!"

The other furrowed her eyebrows and just asked, "Where did you go? We thought you'd slid off the roof, but all we found were Judith's slippers."

"I—" Hani started. She couldn't explain it to them. She didn't even want to try. She just said, "I don't know." The Sisters were not pleased with her explanation.

2014, October 6th, Monday

"Well, they weren't happy, but they seemed to accept my total lie about caring for my sick aunt in Portland," Hani said. She'd just returned from dropping off her paperwork and work ID badge at the local Social Security Office downtown. They'd returned to Rob's condo Sunday night. Hani didn't mind having only a single day of a weekend since she was likely to never work again.

"Didn't want to totally burn your bridges, hunh?" Rob asked.

"Yeah, I like being prepared," Hani replied.

"Oh totally. Not a criticism at all," Rob smiled. "So, can you tell me now what you wanted to practice?"

"Yeah, okay. So, after telling you about the orphanage roof, I spent a while trying to remember all the details about it, the car crash, and some other things. With the car crash, I certainly retained my forward momentum. Thinking about the roof, though, made me realize that while I did seem to have the same retention of my forward slide momentum when I stopped skipping, I had also moved down. Was that gravity?"

"Hmm," Rob considered.

"I don't think it was, because otherwise wouldn't I have sunken into the floor of the cabin while I skipped over Saturday?" Hani pointed out.

"Maybe you know there's nothing but solid planet between you and the core when you were standing in the kitchen?" Rob guessed.

"Yeah, I have no idea, but I have a few tests I'd like to try," Hani said.

"Let's do it," Rob said, still excited that Hani was real.

For the first test, Hani inspected Rob's bed and then asked him to help her peel the mattresses off it. They stacked them against one wall. Hani went and collected a few mixing bowls from the kitchen and returned. Rob scratched his head.

Hani lifted each corner of the bed frame, placing a mixing bowl upside down under each foot.

"What in the world?" Rob asked, holding one side of the bed frame up while Hani placed the last bowl.

"I'm going to lie on the slats of your bed frame and start skipping. I want to see if I drift through the slats into the space under the bed. There wasn't enough room, so I raised the bed," Hani explained.

"Okay, fair enough." Rob nodded. He adjusted his bedside alarm clock so Hani could see it better from where she was going to be.

Hani lay down and said, "Be right back!"

Rob chuffed a laugh as air rushed into where Hani used be with a snap. He wandered out to the living room and carried back a chair. He plucked one of his unfinished books from the bedside table and flipped it open, picking up where he'd left off.

About six hours later, the pages of Rob's book fluttered as Hani thumped back onto his bed slats. Grumpy, she said, "It's not gravity."

"So, I had a thought," Rob said, putting the book down. "You already seem to take the shortest temporal path to safety. You skip bullets, not the whole afternoon, for example. Sliding down the orphanage's roof, though, there was no safe place in the future. A day later, you're still going to be sliding off a roof. You were about to fall, presumably to your death, and the shortest path to safety required physical movement."

"If that's true, then maybe in addition to controlling when I skip, I can control the physical movement too." Hani surmised.

"Yeah, though why did it take you two days to fall through your roof?" Rob asked.

"Maybe it's harder to relocate?" Hani wondered, propping herself uncomfortably up on one elbow. "I've not even tried to think about why I don't go flying off the planet when I skip. If I go shooting forward in time, the planet should have spun away out from under me. It's both spinning on its axis, and spinning around the sun. I wonder why I don't get dumped into space."

"I'm already jealous of your ability. If you can travel to the moon too, I'm out," Rob joked.

Hani got up and started removing the bowls. Rob helped as they reassembled his bed. "I'll try moving in the living room. No need for this crazy setup and keeping you up all night while I try it."

"Good thing I live forever," Rob grinned. "And you're gonna be super easy to feed. You only eat every few days."

"Ha ha," Hani said over her shoulder as she moved into the living room.

They cleared some space in the middle of the room, pulling chairs and the coffee table out of the way. Hani faced the kitchen so she could see the clock. Rob rolled out some masking tape onto the floor behind Hani's heels, marking her starting position.

Rob retreated to his office, saying, "Okay, well, I'll start getting some of the reading done that I've had backlogged." He came back with a stack of books and settled into his chair. "People just keep writing these," Rob joked. "No matter how long I live, I'll never catch up."

"See you later," Hani said and snapped away.

Rob became a blur of page flipping and Hani focused on the remembered sliding sensation as she tried to will herself forward. It was a lot like floating and totally unlike normal physical movement. It was like shifting her perspective, in a way. She always remembered it more like not being able to focus on reading when she was falling asleep at night. She tried to settle into the state, but lost her skipping thread instead.

Rob looked up at the thump. "You're back early!"

"Yeah, hard to focus on two things at once, it seems. Trying again," Hani explained and screwed up her face, trying to snag the thread again. Her view of Rob flicked back to gray again.

Hani tried to visualize a river flowing through the living room. It came from the windows, wound through the furniture, gathered around her, flowed into the open space ahead of her, past Rob, and out into the kitchen. She tried sensing what this push was like instead of trying to pull herself forward. After some focus, the river seemed quite real and she tried to lose her sense of standing on the floor. She wasn't actually standing, but gravity had been such a constant in her life that breaking the illusion was tricky.

She imagined the river becoming heavier and focused on its drag instead of the pretend gravity. Still no shifting of perspective, but she was finding it much harder to hold on to the thread that kept her out of time. Taking this hint, she tried easing up on her grip there and, to her surprise, she felt her vision change very slightly. She held this state and tried to find ways to detect her change of position. From her perspective, just past the edge of her forearm was the leg of one of the chairs. She watched as they became less and less aligned. She crawled forward, propelled by her imagined river. She held the focus, unsure how to make the river "stronger" or herself "lighter."

Meditation would have been a good skill to have developed. This level of focus was extremely hard to maintain. Hani tried to breathe calmly only to discover she wasn't breathing at all, which made that exercise tricky. Instead, she just focused on the slowly shifting elements of the living room. Rob tore through the pages of his book. At some point the daylight went away and Rob flashed to the edge of the room and back, flipping on the room lights. He finished his first book and swapped it for another.

Rob prepared food a few times in the kitchen, but always returned to the chair, reading. As the sun came up, Hani decided to stop. It'd been about 10 minutes, well, hours, and she'd started to really feel exhausted from this.

She thumped into reality again and Rob set down his book. "Oh! Nice! Don't move, I'll get a ruler."

Hani drew several deep cycles of air. "It's so strange, not breathing when I'm skipping."

"I bet! Okay," Rob bent down and measured her heel position against the tape he'd put down before she started her attempt. "One, two, three, four and change. You moved a little over four feet, Hani."

"Exhausting," Hani said, slumping into Rob's now much closer chair.

"You want some breakfast?" Rob suggested.

"Sure, yeah. That would be great," Hani said. "I'm trying to get my eyes working normally again. This was a lot of weird focus with unfocus."

Rob moved to the kitchen and started clanking pans around, preparing eggs, it sounded like. Hani took a few more cleansing breaths and got up, following Rob. She settled onto one of the island stools and watched as he worked.

2014, October 7th, Tuesday

Rob fried up eggs and sausage, threw it across a bed of fresh greens, and added a light oil to top it off. Hani was delighted and chowed down. Rob ate his, continuing to ponder what their purpose was in the world.

Hani paused between bites and asked, "Are you able to change how you look?"

Rob was confused. "What?"

"When you regenerated your hand, you still had body hair on it," Hani pointed to the back of his hand. "There, the hair on the back of your hands. It regrew too. If you regrow hair, then could you grow the hair on your head long, short, whatever you wanted? And if you can do that, what about your face, or your build, your height, your apparent age, or anything?"

Rob was dumb-founded. He'd never considered this at all. He had just assumed that his body restored things to the way they were. "I ... I've never tried, I guess. Everything just comes back the way it's always been."

Hani studied Rob's scalp for a moment. "So if you get a new hair cut and someone comes along and tries to Highlander you, your head pops back out of your neck with the new 'doo?"

Rob looked at her meekly. "I don't really know. I guess it does. I've never tested it. I've never thought to even question it. I mean, my hair does grow and when I get a haircut it doesn't come rushing back out of my head. I guess I've just been distracted when getting injured."

Hani nodded. "Well, I got over the potential threat of death to test my ability. But skipping doesn't hurt me at all. Testing your ability seems rather horrible from a pain perspective."

Rob shrugged, "Yeah, true, but ... I don't know, it's always still a shock, but it goes away so quickly." Rob got up and fetched the butcher knife from his previous demonstration.

"You want to test it now?" Hani asked between bites of her meal.

"Yeah, why not?" Rob slid the cutting board over.

Hani put down her fork, "Wait, wait. What's your plan? I've got some ideas here."

"Sure, what're you thinking?" Rob set the knife down.

"Do you have scissors?" Hani asked.

"Yeah, one moment," Rob leaned over to the knife block and plucked out his kitchen scissors.

"Okay, let me see your hand," Hani said, reaching for Rob's left hand. She studied it for a moment, then took out her phone and took a picture of the back of his hand. She continued, "Right, now, snip off the hair on the back of your pinky finger."

Rob did so. The few strands of hair between his hand and first knuckle drifted to the table.

Hani stared at his hand, "Nope, didn't grow back. Okay, lose the finger!" Hani grinned, "I wasn't ever expecting to say that. I think I have to join the Yakuza or something now."

"I pay tribute!" Rob joked as he reached for his knife again and clipped his pinky onto the cutting board. He grimaced briefly. His replacement pinky sprung from his hand and he wiggled it.

Hani bent closer and examined his hand again, "Your hair grew back! Were you expecting it to grow back?"

"I was, yeah," Rob said, pondering for a moment.

"Do it again, but see if you can try it without wanting it to grow back," Hani suggested.

Rob clipped the hair from his pinky again, took a close look, trying to memorize what it looked like. He kept a close eye on his finger while he put his weight down again, through his joint. "Owww," he said, trying to keep his focus. He pulled his hand away from the knife and watched his new finger pop out. The hair stayed clipped this time.

"Haa!" Hani yelled and clapped him on the back. "You did it! Okay, now try to regrow it! Think of it like an injury!"

Rob focused again. He studied his other pinky for a moment and then back to his left hand. He tried to sense the wrongness of the short hair and felt a little tickle as the hair reestablished its desired length. "Oh wow," was all he managed.

"Nice!" Hani said. She looked up at him and said, "Man, I want you to try to go crazy growing your hair out now. Instant hippie!"

Rob chuckled. "Yeah, no. Let me try growing a beard instead. Here, follow me." Rob got up and went to the bathroom mirror. He stared at his chin and squinted his eyes in concentration. After a few seconds, he felt it. His beard puffed out of his face and he laughed. Hani joined in.

"Instant hobo!" Hani appraised.

"Great, I can make an infinite amount of the worst smelling kindling of all time," Rob observed. He reached for his razor, but Hani stopped him.

"Wait, can you ditch the hair now that you've got it?" she challenged.

Rob stared back at himself in the mirror and tried to think about his regular clean-shaven look. He imagined passing the razor over his cheek, what it felt like, how he looked. His beard went limp and some hair fluttered to the floor. He raised his brows in surprise and then wiped away the remaining hair.

"Awesome," Hani concluded. "You're going to save a fortune on razor blades."

Rob grew silent for a moment. "I wonder if I could age myself. I've looked like this for so long. I'm not sure how I could test that."

"Well, no reason to rush. Maybe you can meditate on it. Or trying changing your shoe size or something easier to visualize," Hani suggested.

Rob nodded. "Actually, there's something I've wanted to test with your abilities that is very similar to this. It's something I noticed pretty early but, since I had no idea what we were dealing with, I kind of put it off."

Hani was curious now. "Oh?"

"Yeah. It's something I wish I could do, as it's been quite a bother whenever I've gotten myself into serious trouble," Rob started to explain. "I only regenerate my body. When you skip, you don't leave your clothes in a pile. How's that possible?"

Hani stared at Rob. It was her turn to be dumb-founded now. "You got me. I never considered it. It's just always been that way. Even when—" she trailed off, thinking of the first time she skipped.

Rob continued, "I didn't want you to think I was creepy or anything." Rob affected a fake drawl, "Hey baby, have ya tried leaving yer clothes behind when you do that thing?"

Hani laughed.

Rob resumed his regular speaking voice, "I actually think trying to add objects would be the real trick."

Hani grinned, "You're not creepy. Besides, we're all adults here."

"Not that I need it," Rob explained, "but if you can take new objects with you, you'd be one hell of a thief. You could just skip through a bank vault, appear, snag some sacks of money, and skip back through the wall carrying them."

Hani nodded in agreement absently. She was distracted by her memories. "Rob, what about the slippers?"

"What?" Rob had no idea.

"My roommate's slippers at the orphanage," Hani recounted, "I always thought they'd just fallen off. But what if I just didn't take them with me? They weren't mine after all."

"Oooh," Rob nodded. "Yeah. Here, let's try it."

Rob led Hani back out of the bathroom, through the living room, and into the front hallway. He opened the hallway closet and extracted a knit hat, handing it to Hani.

"A hat?" Hani turned the hat over in her hands a few times. It looked warm, but she figured that wasn't the point.

"Yeah, see if you can skip with the hat on. And if that works, see if you can skip without bringing the hat along," Rob proposed.

Hani pulled the hat over her head with both hands and said, "Let's ride." She dragged the world to gray and kept a grip on the hat. She popped back into time. Rob was awfully patient.

"Well that worked," Rob observed. "Now the other way. I'll catch it."

Hani thought hard about the hat not belonging to her and how wearing it didn't mean anything. She wanted it off her head. She held the image of herself without the hat and tugged lightly on the skipping thread. She saw a gray Rob flash forward and back from her position and she eased herself back into the hallway.

Rob was standing with his arm outstretched, brandishing the knit hat. "You're a natural at this."

Hani grinned back at him. She really could be a master criminal. Except that it would take her probably weeks to float in and back out of a bank vault. "I want to know my limits on this one."

Rob stepped into the living room, surveying its contents. He pointed at the couch. "Take the whole couch."

Hani's eyes went wide considering it. "I guess ... but what's the limit? Could I take a house? A city? One way to find out, I guess." She brushed a few throw pillows to the side and took a seat in the center of the couch. She spread her arms out across the back of the couch and tried to reach her senses out over it. She was driving it, like a car.

Besides cars, she'd ridden horses, pedaled bikes, aimed skis, you name it. All of those things became second nature when piloting them. They were just extensions of her own body. How else could people drive in traffic? The vehicle is just a big metal suit to slip into. Hani figured this was why giant Mecha robots seem like such a natural and plausible science fiction element. Humans excelled at extending their somatic motor-sensory systems beyond their physical body.

She closed her eyes while thinking about the space and texture of the couch. How it would be hard to maneuver through the living room, even if it had wheels. Her eyelids became see-through to a gray world and she felt an odd weight on her mind. That was new, so she released her grip on the skip.

The magazines and books on the coffee table got blown away from her onto the floor and she heard the blinds on the windows behind her flapping. Rob had raised his hands, shielding his face, in a needless instinctive defensive move. He lowered them and said simply, "Damn."

"Oh my God. That worked, didn't it?" Hani said, almost jumping to her feet.

"Yeah, it sure did. That was a hell of an air displacement, too. That's a lot more volume than before," Rob said, picking up a few of the fallen books. "I hope no one calls the cops on us. That sounded like I tipped my fridge over. Twice."

"It did feel different. I can only come up with weight analogies, but the whole thing just felt heavier," Hani said. She moved over to the wall and gripped the corner between her thumb and forefinger. She tried to imagine the structure of the building.

"Wait wait! Not the building! What'll happen to the pipes and wiring?" Rob exclaimed.

Hani couldn't find the thread, it was slipping around and she couldn't move fast enough to catch it. She stabbed after it and felt the building drop away from her. She aborted and came back to the world.

Rob was frowning. "Well, at least we know you can't take a whole building with you. Thankfully."

Hani nodded. "Or buildings aren't meant to be driven," she mused half to herself.

Rob studied her for a moment. "Do we need to go to the garage? There's plenty to drive there." He took out his keys and jingled them enticingly.

Hani took a deep breath. "Okay, sure."

They left the condo and waited for the elevator in silence. On the way to the garage Rob said, "If this works, it's really going to make a lot of noise. We should probably drive somewhere outside."

Hani nodded, "Like where I won't set off 20 car alarms at the same time?"

"Yeah, exactly. I'm kind of worried about busting glass too. The air displacement from the couch almost knocked me down. I can't imagine what it's going to be like for a whole car," Rob said. "I think I've actually got a place in mind. It's pretty close but industrial enough that no one should be around to bother us."

They got in the Jeep and Rob drove up out of the garage to street level. He wound his way through the Pearl, got on I405 briefly, then took US30 west, heading out along the Columbia. After about ten minutes of driving, he turned off US30 and started down some side streets through a sprawling industrial zone. It looked like storage facilities for the docks closer to the river.

"There are some unused industrial parks just south of the city dump out here," Rob explained. "I spent some time exploring the buildings a few months ago."

"Exploring?" Hani asked, suspecting this was just a partial story.

"Well, I was also practicing my lock-picking skills, but yeah, exploring. I just wanted to see what all that space had been used for," Rob answered. He turned left into the deserted parking lot. "Here seems as good a place as any. We've got some bushes lining the lot and empty buildings on two sides."

Rob got out and left the driver's side door open. Hani swung open the passenger door and walked around to the driver's side. She hopped in and looked over at Rob, who'd taken several paces backward from the Jeep.

"You afraid you're gonna get hurt?" Hani joked.

"Hey, I might cut my fingers off at the drop of a hat, but this stuff still stings," Rob replied in mock offense.

Hani closed her eyes again and settled her mind. She felt the seat belt across her chest and hips. She felt the finger width indentations in the steering wheel and imagined driving the Jeep. A bumper behind her, a bumper in front. The car was her outer shell now.

The world went gray, but she knew immediately it hadn't worked. The Jeep wasn't semi-translucent like her body was while she was skipping. She plopped back into time and turned to Rob, saying, "Gimme a second." She started the Jeep and drove it around in a few circles and figure eights. She could feel the tires, the air through the open window. Much better.

She stopped the Jeep back near Rob again and then went fishing for the edge of her mind. As the world snapped gray, she felt a giant weight on her. If she had needed to breathe while skipping, she wouldn't have been able to. If she was trying to remember a phone number, it would have been blotted out. She could barely keep enough sense to let go of her skipping.

She heard an echoing pop rattle back from the industrial park building walls. Rob had covered his ears instinctively. She couldn't quite see straight and the Jeep felt like it was spinning. She opened the door and staggered out of the Jeep, catching herself before she almost tumbled to the ground. Rob rushed over and hoisted her back to a sitting position against the edge of the driver's seat.

"Whoa, you okay there?" Rob asked, looking back and forth between her eyes.

"Ugh," Hani offered. "I feel like I'm gonna puke."

"Well, we're done for now. You stole my Jeep just fine, but you look terrible—" Rob trailed off and reached past Hani to the center console. He fetched a spare napkin, saved from the fast food stop they'd made on the way back from the cabin. Hani flinched slightly as Rob pressed the napkin to her philtrum and placed her hand over the napkin. "You've got a nose bleed."

Hani spent a few minutes recovering. The bleed had stopped pretty quickly, but was still rather alarming. "I guess this really is like trying to hold my breath."

Rob, still looking worried, said, "What?"

"You know, if skipping is like breathing. If I tried to hold my breath too long, I'd just pass out and start breathing again. I think this is the same. I'd pass out—"

"Or worse" Rob interjected.

"Or worse, maybe. But it'd stop, regardless," Hani finished.

"This addition to your skill should maybe be trained in smaller increments," Rob suggested.

"Yeah, no battleships for me yet," Hani agreed. She felt better now. She handed Rob the car keys, walked around to the passenger side, and climbed back into the Jeep. "I could use some lunch, actually."

Rob slammed his door shut and put the keys back in the ignition. "That sounds like a great plan."

Hani looked at Rob for a moment and got a new idea. She reached for his hand on the stick shift and took hold of him. In an instant she dragged this friend of hers into the gray. He was translucent and unmoving. The sun shifted a bit above her and she relaxed, dropping them back into existence.

Rob looked at her hand and then up at her face. "What's up? You okay?"

"Oh wow, you didn't see it, did you?" Hani said, surprised.

"See what?" Rob asked.

"Look at the time," Hani pointed to the clock on the Jeep's dash.

Rob stared at the time, puzzled.

"I just skipped, but I brought you with," Hani admitted.

Rob's eyes went wide. "A thief and now a kidnapper! Also, Jesus, you just nearly broke yourself taking the Jeep on a ride. You sure you're alright?"

"A kidnapper," Hani repeated slowly. "'Entführer', in German."

1940

Some of the other children called the guards "Entführer," which didn't make a lot of sense to her. She didn't remember what the beginning meant, but the end of the word meant "leader." They did seem in charge, but they couldn't all be the leader. Her parents had mentioned something about the "Führer" before, and the guards seemed to wear the same costume, so she figured they were on the same team. She thought her parents hadn't liked this Leader, but Hani wasn't really sure what was happening.

Hani didn't understand why she had to stay with the other children. She and her parents had already been forced to leave their home and travel here, and now she couldn't even stay with them. Her parents had said they'd see her again shortly, but it didn't feel true.

When she'd first arrived, she'd wandered around the new room for a while and went looking for a place to set down her doll, but all the beds were taken. After a few minutes, she began to tear up. There was no place for her and her parents still weren't back.

"What's your name?" An older girl asked her.

"Hanielle," Hani replied.

"I'm Eva. You can stay here with me, if you want," Eva offered, patting the end of her bed.

"Okay," Hani sniffed and she settled in, not sure what to do next. She stared at her doll for a while and stroked its hair.

After a few days, Hani pretty well agreed with her parents. If these guards were with The Leader, then he was telling them bad things. She and the other children barely ate and never got to go outside. There was a tiny toilet near the back but it was disgusting. Hani hated it here. Everyone hated it here.

To pass the time, she decided to teach her doll to count. Before they'd come here, she'd just been taught about how tens and hundreds worked. She'd had no problem counting to one hundred, and she was pleased with how things just repeated again. One hundred and one, one hundred and two. She helped her doll count the girls in the dorm with her. There were 112 of them. She counted the beds, they had 50 bunk beds. Counting to 50 twice got her to 100. It meant 12 beds were shared. Currently, anyway.

There'd been more girls earlier. Sometimes the guards would come in and pick out one or two and leave with them. Hani had assumed they were going back home since they never came back to the dorm.

Yesterday, however, a fight broke out when the guards tried to take another girl. She didn't want to go and a few others tried to stop the guards. The guards hit them with their guns and took the girl anyway. Hani really did not like the guards.

Today, the guards arrived again and marched through the dorm, looking for something. Everyone tried to avoid eye contact. Hani pulled her sheet up to her neck and hid her doll under the covers.

As they approached, one of the guards looked at her. He stopped at her row and called to the others, "This one will do."

Hani's eyes went wide and Eva got up, standing between Hani and the guards, shouting at them, "Go to hell. Leave her alone. I won't let you—"

The guard shoved Eva to the ground, "Shut your mouth, filth."

The other guards had their guns out, ready for anyone else that might object. The first guard grabbed Hani by the arm and dragged her out of bed. She fought, trying to twist out of his grip. He picked her off the ground and tossed her over his shoulder. She flailed in the air, beating his back with her fists and her only weapon: her doll. He ignored her protestations and retreated from the dorm.

The other guards followed him out but stayed behind at the outside of the dorm. Hani's captor continued on to the larger building near the center of the camp. She'd stopped flailing and just waited. They made their way into the building and the guard went down a few flights of stairs.

As they walked through the hallway he'd chosen, Hani saw a bunch of people sleeping on cots. They were along both walls of the hallway. It seemed a terrible place to try to take a nap. Besides the chilly temperature, people clearly walked through the halls. That was an entirely unpeaceful environment for catching up on sleep. Maybe that's why they had all pulled their sheets up over their faces.

The guard stepped through one of the doors along the hallway and set Hani down. She held her doll close and looked around the tiled room. A man in a thin long white coat was hunched over a table at one end of the room. The other end of the room had just a chair.

"Delivery, Doctor," the guard intoned.

The other man waved his hand behind him toward the guard, "Yes, thank you. Strap her in."

The guard hesitated, "The straps are too big for her. Shall I stay?"

The man shook his head, annoyed, "No, just wait outside."

The guard clicked his heels together and exited the room. Hani heard the door latch behind him. She looked around, but there wasn't much to see. The walls were all white tile, just like the floor. The ceiling was concrete, like most of the rest of the buildings, and punctuated with lights every few feet. In the center of the room was a large drain, like it had come out of a huge bathtub. Hani looked around for faucets, but saw only a single hose rolled up in the near corner at the end of the room with the table and the man.

The man finished what he was doing and turned to look at Hani. "Ah, very good. You'll be perfect." He smiled.

Hani didn't believe that was a real smile. He reminded her of the creepier guards.

"Please have a seat," he gestured to the chair.

Hani considered her options and decided it was a reasonable enough request. She walked to the chair in a few small steps and sat down. The chair had weird buckles on the arm rests. Hani ignored them and set her doll on her lap.

"Now, you're here to help me test a ... new toy we found," the man stepped to the side to show off the table's contents. In the center was a large movie projector like the one Hani's father had shown her when they went to see a film last year. Her father knew the projectionist, who showed them around the film booth. He'd been a coworker before her father had to get a different job. Her father had been very angry with the Reichsfilmkammer, but Hani didn't understand why.

Next to the projector were several thin sheets of material on stands. The man continued, "I want to shine different color lights on you. It will only take a few moments."

"Why?" Hani asked.

The man looked startled and after a moment said, "I want to understand the toy we found." He crouched down and came eye-level with another object on a stand. This one looked like a broken shard from a bowl. Hani could see some writing on it, but she was too far away to make it out.

"We found it years ago, but only recently did I unlock its true capabilities." He stared at it for a while and then straightened up. "Ready?"

"Where are my parents?" Hani demanded. "I want to go home."

The man shook his head, "No, no, sorry, that's not possible. Now, sit still." He flipped on the projector. The light focused on the broken bowl shard which started to glow slightly. Initially, the shard cast a large shadow directly over Hani. After a few seconds, the shard's glow began to throb and a faint light shown out of it, filling the area of the shadow, illuminating Hani. It wasn't very bright, but Hani didn't like it anyway.

"I have to use the bathroom," Hani said.

"Hold still," the man said and started sliding different colored gels between the projector and the shard.

The glow on her felt like a weird breeze. It wasn't cold, it wasn't warm, but she got goosebumps anyway. The breeze changed with each new color. The man wrote on a clipboard between each color shift, glancing up at her briefly.

"I want to see my parents," Hani demanded again.

The man got upset, "You can't see them, now stay still." He continued writing.

Hani got up and ran to the door. She yanked on it, but it was locked. The man looked up from his notes and yelled, "No! Get back in the chair you stupid little girl!"

Hani snarled at him and threw her doll at his face. He stumbled, but caught it. She'd closed the distance between them and kicked him in the shin as hard as she could. The girls had taught her that move on the second day. They said she had to do it to anyone she wanted to get away from. It seemed to be working, since the man was now howling in pain, and had dropped her doll and slapped the clipboard off the table in his effort to keep his balance.

Hani picked up her doll and decided to steal his toy too.

"Guards!" the man had started yelling.

Hani heard the door behind her burst open, but she kept moving. She reached up and snatched the shard from its stand and turned to face the man again. The man had backed up against the wall and his eyes were filled with fear, just like the eyes of the girls they'd taken before her. The guards had their guns unslung, pointed at her.

"Quick, quick," the man yelled pointing at her. "Kill her before she explodes like the others!"

Hani had wanted to get away, but suddenly she couldn't move. The lights in the room had changed again. Everything was gray and all the men were gone. There was no sound at all. She struggled to move, but quickly gave up. She wasn't scared. She felt quite relaxed, actually. She saw streaks of motion in the room that came and went. She didn't understand what was happening.

Her bladder urgency was gone too. She could see she was still holding the shard and her doll. She couldn't let go, so she just waited. She seemed to be getting taller, but after a while she realized she was floating.

Over the next hour or so, she'd floated up out of the building and through the walls. She assumed this was a dream—a very strange dream. She hoped her mother would wake her up soon. She didn't like the man with the lights.

Outside she noticed that the sun was moving quickly through the sky. It had never worked like that before. At night, the stars came out. During the day, guards flashed through the compound, vehicles arrived and disappeared noiselessly, and sometimes lots of people would march through the street at high speed.

By the seventh day, she realized she'd been counting the sun's transits. She'd watched as many days as she was years old. She continued to wait. It had been a while now. Almost as long as the movie she'd seen the day her father showed her the projectionist's booth. The floating continued as she passed through the corner of another building during the night. This one was filled with adults. She could make them out while they slept. They looked very thin.

She floated through open ground, through a vehicle depot, a garden, an office building, and a barracks. She'd counted to nine hundred now and wasn't sure how to continue past 999. She made up a solution and considered it ten one hundreds and continued her count of the sun passing overhead. It felt like an entire normal day had gone by and she was starting to get exceedingly bored.

Around the count of 13 hundreds, she noticed a tall fence that stretched in both directions around the compound. She was drifting toward the large gate that all the vehicles came and went through. She continued to count.

She finished passing through the gate as the sun came up on count 18 hundreds and 54. She felt like she should have gone to bed a few hours ago, but she wasn't tired. She noticed some new types of vehicles were parked outside the gate. Suddenly, all of the color returned to the world.

1945, April 29th

Several men in uniforms, different from the camp guards, turned and looked over at Hani. They seemed briefly confused, but one approached and spoke to her. She didn't understand him, but he didn't look angry. She held her doll tightly and kept a firm grip on her shard of pottery.

The man bent down to meet her at eye level, saying, "My German is poor. Name is Marvin."

Hani studied him for a few moments and replied, "My name is Hanielle."

"Good day, Hanielle," Marvin said. He beckoned to someone in one of the cars. A woman emerged from a van and walked briskly over to them. She and the man talked for a few moments. Hani heard her own name mentioned and kept watching them.

"Hello Hanielle," the woman said. "I'm Gretta. Marvin said he just found you out here? Were you in the camp?"

Hani nodded her head. Marvin stood up, smiled at Hani, waved, and retreated to where he'd been standing before. "I want to go home," Hani said.

"Yes, I'm going to help with that, Hanielle. It may take us a while. There are many more people like you that need to go home. They were all taken from their homes, like you. We're here to help all of you." Gretta knelt down and started inspecting Hani lightly. "Are you hurt?"

"I have to pee," Hani admitted.

"Okay, let's go take care of that," Gretta answered. She stood and offered her hand for Hani to hold. Hani shifted her doll around, stuffing her under her other arm, keeping a grip on her shard, and took Gretta's hand.

Gretta turned toward the open gates of the camp, but Hani stopped in her tracks. She did not want to go back that way. She'd just gotten out.

"It's okay, Hanielle. All the bad men have been stopped," Gretta pointed to the line of guards against one of the trucks. Their hands were bound and none of them had any guns. The men dressed like Marvin had the guns now and were searching the guards, loading them into the truck. "There's a bathroom in the gate house," Gretta explained.

Hani relented and allowed Gretta to guide her toward the gate house.

Later that day, Hani had gone for a long ride back to a different camp. Gretta had explained this camp was being used to help all the other people from the Nazi camp. Hani had learned that was the name the bad men used. The new camp was run by the United States Army. Hani had heard of the United States before. Many of the guards at this camp were dressed like Marvin. Hani was relieved to see that these guards numbered very few and mostly seemed to be looking out of the camp instead of into it.

Gretta brought Hani to be checked in. Hani joined a short line of other girls. When she got to the front they asked her for her full name, where she was from, her parent's names, and other questions she didn't entirely understand, but she did her best. She had to be checked for lice, they explained, and she consented, but didn't want to give up her doll and shard.

They offered her new clothes and one of the older girls helped her get changed. Hani still didn't put down her shard, though she did have to let go of her doll to get the dress over her head. She settled into her own cot in the new dorm.

"But my parents can find me?" Hani asked one of the girls as she was getting ready for bed.

The girl nodded. She seemed sad. "That's what they're doing here. They're finding our families."

Hani wasn't entirely satisfied, but tried to sleep anyway. She dreamed of the gray world. It wasn't the same, though, since that world had no sound, but her dreams were filled with all the noises from the old camp.

Over the next few days, Hani relaxed a bit more and made a few new friends. Over lunch, one of them, Elsa, asked Hani about her pottery shard.

"What is it?" Elsa inquired.

"I don't know," Hani admitted. "I took it from the Nazis. They didn't want me to have it and they wanted me to sit still, but I got out." Hani held it out for the table to see.

"It has writing on it?" Elsa said, pointing at the more polished side.

"I can't read it," Hani said, shrugging.

"Can I see it?" Elsa asked.

Hani hesitated. She put it down on the table gently and looked around. Nothing changed. No Nazis stormed in. She nodded and slid it toward Elsa.

Elsa reached for the shard and as her fingers touched it, the shard flashed brightly and Elsa was thrown backwards across the aisle and into several other children eating at the neighboring table. Talking stopped and everyone turned to see what was happening. The other kids picked themselves up and tried to help Elsa, but she was limp.

Hani's eyes were wide with terror. The other kids at her table looked from Elsa back to the shard, uncertain about what they'd just seen. A few adults hurried over. One man said, "What's going on here?"

An Army man with a red cross on his arm, instead of the swastika Hani had grown used to, crouched down to examine Elsa while the other adults continued to demand details.

"That thing," one of the girls at Hani's table offered, "it zapped her."

"What?" the first man asked, confused.

"She's just unconscious," the Army man said.

Hani reached for the shard, but the first man interrupted her motion, "Ah! Nobody moves until I know who did this."

"It was my pottery," Hani tried to explain.

The man looked at the shard and back to Hani. The other children nodded.

"My father had that happen to him when he was repairing our light fixture once," one of the boys offered. "It looked just like that. He fell off the ladder and we had to get the doctor."

The man screwed up his face in a frustrated combination of confusion and disbelief. He looked under the table, under the bench, and went down on one knee to check the floor. Nothing was out of place or weird. He stood up and stared at the shard for a moment.

He leaned over and took a pen out of the Army man's jacket's front pocket and poked the shard with it. It rotated slightly, just like a broken fragment of pottery might be expected to. He swapped the pen to his other hand, took a handkerchief from his back pocket, and picked up the shard without touching it directly.

Hani squirmed uncomfortably. She might need that again, if it really was what saved her. What if these children weren't as nice as the others? What if these Army men didn't let them go? She watched the man carefully, looking for an opportunity to get her shard back.

"Just looks like part of a bowl," the man stated to no one in particular. He waved at another adult, beckoning him over, "Hey Frank, check this out."

Frank approached and adjusted his glasses slightly, leaning in to study the artifact in the first man's hand, cradled by the handkerchief.

"Is that Hebrew writing?" Frank asked.

"Maybe?" offered the first man, unhelpfully.

"May I?" Frank asked.

Elsa groaned and the Army man helped her up to a seated position.

"It's your life," the first man said, glancing worriedly at Elsa and back to the shard.

Frank reached out a hand and tried to scoop the shard from the handkerchief. Just like with Elsa, he got blasted down the aisle and skidded limply to a stop on the ground. A few kids jumped up on their bench, trying to get out of the way of Frank's splayed limbs.

"Holy shit," the Army man said, rushing down the aisle to tend to Frank.

The first man had recaptured the pottery shard in his handkerchief after it had been bumped by Frank. He gaped at it and lowered his hands slightly, unconsciously trying to move this unknown danger away from his face. He turned to look at his compatriot.

"Not dead," declared the Army man. "Pulse is a little erratic, though." The Army man rolled up his jacket and put it under Frank's head.

Hani took this opportunity with the first man not paying attention to her and plucked the shard from the handkerchief. The crowd that had gathered around them gasped in unison, but Hani held on to it without issue and sat back down on the bench.

The first man's attention had snapped back to Hani and everyone watched her resume eating her meal. The man stuffed his handkerchief clumsily back into his pocket and said, "Okay, everyone. Show's over." He leaned in to Hani saying, "What's your name?"

"Hanielle," Hani said with her mouth full.

"Everyone please don't touch Hanielle's trinket. It's, uh, a bit temperamental," the man struggled.

Hani finished her meal while the crowd slowly dispersed. The man left, instructing the other adults to keep an eye on Hani and to report back to him when Frank came to.

Over the next few days, Hani got a lot of attention because of that meal's events. The other people in the camp wanted to see the fragment. No one wanted to touch it, especially those that had seen first-hand what it did to Elsa and Frank. One adult saw the writing and said he'd be back with a friend, Bruriah.

Bruriah arrived later that day. Hani was surprised at how old she was. She couldn't remember any of her fellow camp members having been much older than her parents. Bruriah asked Hani to hold the shard up to the light for her to see better.

Bruriah frowned slowly and looked at Hani who was grinning proudly while holding the object firmly in her finger tips.

"Life," she said to Hani after a moment longer of study.

"Life?" Hani asked.

"This word says 'life,'" Bruriah said. "I can't make out what the others say. They're off the edges of this fragment. Maybe 'peace,'" she lied.

"That's ironic," said one of the adults that had come with Bruriah.

Bruriah leveled her gaze at the man. "Do not presume to understand our world."

The man didn't reply and Bruriah turned to Hani saying, "You must release this object. It has already led us from the darkness. It's purpose to you is at an end, child."

Hani didn't really understand, but nodded in agreement. As Bruriah retreated with her entourage, the shard got slowly warmer in Hani's hand. She set it down on the trunk at the foot of her cot before it got too hot. After the onlookers had dissipated, Hani reached for the fragment again. She held it, but it was still uncomfortably hot.

The dinner bell rang and she left it behind.

2014, October 7th, Tuesday

The look on Rob's face stopped Hani from continuing to recount her childhood. They'd gotten back to the condo while she'd been telling him how she'd escaped from Dachau. Rob looked upset, like he'd seen a ghost.

"What color was it?" Rob asked.

"The fragment?" Hani tried to clarify.

"Yes. Do you remember the details?" Rob asked intently. He was leaning in, much more focused, without his commonly relaxed posture.

"It was an earthy red on the side with the writing," Hani tried to remember. "It had a smooth finish, but the surface was somewhat uneven. The writing was pale and etched into the surface probably before it was fired. The reverse side was similar, but with a lighter color. A white beige, with small ridges running in the same direction as the writing. It didn't have the glazed finish, though."

Rob sat back slightly on his stool and his gaze shifted away. They hadn't put the living room back together since the earlier experiments, so they'd settled in the kitchen again.

Rob focused back on Hani, "What happened to it?"

"Well, I remember that a bunch of different people came by every few days to examine it. I got pretty creeped out by some of the later ones, since they were wearing lab coats. It wasn't their fault; they had no idea what I'd seen in the other camp. Apparently all scientists wear white lab coats or something," Hani recounted. "Some of them tried to pick it up and it was always the same result. They got tossed across the room. And they'd always ask me to pick it up and all it did was get hot while I held it.

"Eventually they packed me up to come to America. I remember they were careful to put it in a box and to have me carry it. I was getting pretty sick of the thing by now. I was well fed, warm, and people were nice, if a little standoffish, about the pottery. I felt safe, but I missed my parents still.

"Some of the other girls tried to explain to me that my parents were probably dead. That didn't go over well, as you might imagine. It started the seed of doubt in my mind, but I held on to the hope that they'd come find me. I cried when they told me I had to leave the camp for America.

"The US soldiers were all super sweet with me. I remember they played games with me on the plane ride and they had a bunch of coloring books for me too. They were coloring in them with me. Man, I wish I had those. Remembering back to it now, I suspect there was some seriously not-age-appropriate stuff going on in the pages they were drawing, but they never showed me. We just all sat around coloring," Hani recalled.

"And the box with the fragment came with you?" Rob tried to direct the conversation back to his concern.

"Yeah. When we landed, they took the box and I had all kinds of medical exams. They figured out pretty quick I didn't like lab coats. They still bother me, actually. But they were perfectly nice, gentle. All the nurses were great with me, though the language difference really started to become a problem. They cycled through a handful of translators during the first few months.

"After a while, when they were done touring me around the

Army base there in Massachusetts, they transferred me to an orphanage closer to Boston ... the Emerson School for Children. I had a woman from the Army check in with me every few months, but I never saw the box or the fragment again," Hani concluded.

Rob looked somber. He took a deep breath and explained his mood, "What you've described is alarmingly similar to an object I'm quite familiar with. If it is the same one, then we need to recover it. It should not fall into the wrong hands. And most hands are wrong, unfortunately."

"I haven't thought about it in years," Hani admitted. "I've never entirely been sure any of those things really happened. It was so long ago now and the whole event seemed like some surreal nightmare."

"You said a woman checked in with you while you were at the orphanage? Do you remember her name?" Rob inquired, forging ahead in his quest.

"Actually, yeah, she was German too," Hani wracked her brain. "Miss Schiffer. Vanda? I think it was Vanda Schiffer."

"Do you still have access to your Social Security databases?" Rob asked.

"Probably," Hani guessed. "The IT guys are usually pretty backed up." Hani paused and tried to read Rob's face. "Rob, she's probably dead. The last time she visited was before I started high school. That would have been ... 1954," Hani calculated. "She was an adult and it's been 60 years."

"We have to try," Rob said flatly.

"Okay, sure, I'm game. I want to see what you're after." Hani went to the hallway and fetched her satchel, bringing it back to the kitchen. She pulled out her laptop and got set up to log in to her office.

Rob looked worried. He was fidgeting.

"Okay, I'm in. Looks like they're about a week behind on their ticket queue. Let me see ... Massachusetts, Schiffer. A few hits," Hani narrated while clicking away on her touchpad. "Hmm, no Vanda. Let me check name changes, one second. Ah, okay, she married in 1955. Vanda Engel. Alright, long history of government employment. She started drawing in 1997 and she's still kicking. She's 91, Rob."

"Where is she?" Rob persisted.

"Looks like a retirement community in Arizona," Hani said, bringing up a Google search result quickly.

Rob leaned over Hani's shoulder to read with her. Hani hadn't noticed him produce his cell phone, but he was already dialing. After a moment, she could hear it ringing.

"Hello, my name is Robert. I wanted to arrange a visit with one of your residents ... Yes ... Vanda Engel ... No ... I'm traveling through the area with an old friend of hers from Massachusetts and we'd love to stop in and see her ... I understand ... Of course, her name is Hanielle Gittel. She was one of Ms Engel's wards at the Emerson School for Children."

Rob left his number with them and hung up.

"What'd they say?" Hani asked.

"They said they'd ask her if she wanted to see us and would call us back," Rob said. "I'm not waiting, though." He paused and looked at Hani. "Will you come with me? I'll get us airfare to Phoenix. We must find a way to talk with her."

"Sure. I never thought I'd see her again," Hani admitted.

1310

It had been almost a whole season since Johannes had left England. He'd been traveling with his brothers-in-arms for most of the time. He thought frequently of Isabel, but he had to assume she wasn't going to wait for him. She was young and he had dedicated himself to God. It didn't mean he couldn't marry, but all the crusading was going to make that pretty hard.

Other Knights had already reached Egypt to try and protect several critical sites. The Papal decree against the infidels was clear: the able-bodied had to join in the war to defend the relics and regain control of the region. Johannes and his travel mates hadn't yet reached their assigned city, but news continued to trickle back to them through the ports. The skirmishes had been pretty well isolated to the edges of the city and most of the Knights hadn't even had to draw their swords yet.

The trip to Egypt had been long, but mostly uneventful. The boat from Rome had stopped at several ports along the way, each with filled with increasingly stranger sights and smells. The Knights spent most evenings dragging the boat crew out of brothels. They were going to make sure that the sins of their brothers would not stop them from making it to their ultimate destination.

They had a day of travel left and the prior night had been a late one while Johannes and his brother Michael had searched many rooms for the ship's captain. The boat crew really did not appreciate this endless meddling. As a result, the Knights took watch shifts to make sure the boat crew didn't try to murder them in their sleep and pitch them overboard. Johannes wondered if there might have been some more religiously dedicated crews they could have found instead of this group of craven sinners.

Johannes woke to Michael yelling for his attention. Michael crashed through the door to the room they shared at the inn, "Brother! The boat burns! The crew has scattered."

Johannes groaned, "These horrible men. How are they our confederates? They are a different breed and resist any attempts at their salvation. How far are we by horse?"

"We don't have the money for horses," Michael said, frowning.

"There are only 24 of us, Michael. Surely we can find a few carts for hire?" Johannes tried to make plans while getting dressed.

"I will ask the innkeeper," Michael declared, leaving Johannes to finish gathering his armor and belongings.

The Knights organized themselves in front of the inn. Michael had found three cart teams that had agreed to carry them to the next port over land. They'd be using the last of their Papal stipend, but they had all agreed it was the right choice. Their purpose was God's purpose and defending their designated city was top priority.

As the sun crept up into the sky, they started on their way. The driver of Johannes's cart struck up a conversation in broken French, "You are defenders? What are you defending?"

Johannes replied, "We are Knights Templar. We have an oath to defend the interests of God and reinforce His obligations to His people."

"Ah, Templar," the driver acknowledged. "Many of you have headed this way. I have delivered several cart loads of supplies over the last few months. What is so important about this city? It has no seat of power, no library."

"Pope Clement the Fifth has declared it protected. I serve my faith and I serve the Holy Father. It is my duty to obey, not to question," Johannes replied solemnly.

The driver nodded slowly, "All men should question, friend. Any faith that cannot withstand questioning is no true faith."

"My faith is tested regularly, driver," Johannes said defensively.

"I meant no offense, friend," the driver backed down. "I have just found that blind faith can be a curse when you least expect it. I am a religious man, but I must understand my beliefs, or else I cannot know that I am a good man."

Johannes did not reply. The driver stayed silent for the rest of the day.

The caravan took several days to reach its destination. The Knights were exhausted from the road. They parted ways with the drivers, who left to find potential cart loads for the return home. Johannes and his fellow travelers made their way on foot to the reliquary at the center of town. The other Knights greeted them somberly as they approached and helped them carry gear into the make-shift barracks.

Once they were squared away in the meeting hall, Johannes asked the local Knights' Master and Commander, "What news of the Mamluks?"

"We had hoped they'd ignore us and stay busy with the recent Ilkhanate raids to the east, but it seems, instead, we're being viewed as allies to the Mongols. The Mamluks have been massing near the city's border, but we have God on our side," the Commander ended jovially, loudly, so the others could hear him. "Your forces combined with ours will be more than enough to repel them. They have no training and their arrows cannot penetrate our walls."

Michael chimed in, worried, "I have heard they outnumber us four to one. Should we retreat with the artifacts instead?"

"There is too much here, Michael," Johannes explained. "We cannot let these holy objects come under the control of the Vizier. They would come to profane use against God's people."

The Commander studied them carefully. "Michael, Johannes, come with me," he ordered, and walked through the hall to the doors at the back.

Johannes and Michael jumped up and followed their new Commander closely. Through the doors, they turned and ducked into the side corridor that took them to the basement of the reliquary. They walked past cabinets of jars filled with hazy liquid, collections of censors, lamps, monstrances, folded robes, and ornate boxes. Johannes wondered what was out of sight in the drawers.

They wound through the labyrinthine halls. Their Commander stopped every few paces to light a sconce. Judging by the distance walked, Johannes assumed they must have traveled under the barracks, across the roadway above, and were approaching the chapel that was across the street.

"Under the chapel," their Commander confirmed, "is the most protected area of the reliquary." He lit one more torch and they were at a dead-end. Sitting alone on a low table was a small pottery cup. Just below the lip of the cup a dark liquid reflected the flickering lights of the alcove.

The Commander turned to the table and gestured at the cup. "Only the Cup matters."

Michael looked confused.

The Commander continued, "Everything else here, though

precious, is harmless in the hands of the infidels. The Cup, though, has great power. You must protect this with your lives. The rest can fall, but this must be destroyed if we cannot hold the Mamluks."

"I am here to defend God's people," Johannes objected. "My skills are wasted in this crypt. Let me fight alongside my Brothers."

"If we fall, you two are the last defense against the infidels. Swear to me that you will destroy the Cup before it falls into our enemy's hands." Their Commander stared at them in turn.

"But you will not be defeated, Commander," Michael protested. "You said we would crush them handily."

"I have lied, Brother," the Commander admitted. "We are outnumbered forty to one. They are intent on recovering this. They know its power and the Vizier of the Mamluks will stop at nothing to reach it. We only recently learned of their intent. You are dedicated Knights and the last of our kind to reach here. Yesterday, the Mamluks gained control of the port. The other Knights that were coming were sunk in the bay last night. All day today the Mamluks have been unloading even more troops from a fleet that arrived this morning. I prayed to God for reinforcements and your troop arrived on carts, by land. We will hold the reliquary as long as possible, but it is too late for us to flee."

Johannes and Michael stood motionless, shocked into silence.

"But, the road, Commander," Johannes demanded. "We can retreat now, we must find the cart drivers and escape with the Cup."

"The roads have been closed for weeks, Brother. I can only assume the Mamluks let you in on purpose, since they were not yet ready to strike. They must be confident that a couple dozen more Knights will make no difference in their conquest here," the Commander replied.

1310, Fall

The alcove was silent while the truth sunk in. Their attention snapped to the ceiling when they heard the church bell above them begin to ring. The Commander instinctively put a hand on his pommel, saying, "It is time, Brothers. God be with you. I will lead the charge above. You must protect the Cup."

Johannes and Michael turned to look at each other briefly and then nodded to their Commander in unison. The Commander retreated around the corner and they listened to his footsteps as they faded. After the echoes died away, Johannes started looking around the alcove and the adjoining hallway.

"This is not a very defensible position," Michael complained.

"Agreed, but it is tight. It will be hard for them to overwhelm us. With us side by side, this will be mostly one-on-one combat," Johannes calculated.

"Maybe we will never see the Mamluks," Michael hoped.

Johannes investigated his charge. The Cup sat on a white cloth that covered all but the outer inch of the table's surface. The cloth had no markings, but was mostly covered in a thin layer of dust. Extending in a small radius around the Cup's base, there was no dust at all. The exterior of the Cup was glazed with an earthy red/brown. Etched into the side was what looked like Aramaic.

"Brother Michael," Johannes called. "You studied Aramaic? What does the Cup have written on it?"

Michael turned away from his watch on the hallway and crouched in front of the table, examining the etching. "It says, 'Door' ... 'to life'? Well, I'm not sure. It's written alliteratively, suggesting the phrase 'The road of life', but it's not 'road'. The first word means 'entrance', or 'door'. In a religious context, it would be 'rapture.'"

Johannes peered into the Cup. "It's full," he reported.

Michael pondered, "Do they keep it filled? I would expect any contents to diminish, even in this dankness."

"I don't think anyone's been down here in a while," Johannes said, pointing to their footprints in the dust. "This must be a truly blessed artifact."

Michael stood up and they both held their breath. They could hear a noise far away that sounded like the echoes of a blacksmith. "They're coming," Michael said, drawing his sword.

Johannes left his sheathed, no reason to wear out his arm early waiting for them. The time trickled by as the sound of clashing metal continued to get louder. Michael stepped forward into the hall and strained to listen. They could make out the shouting and cursing between the clatter of blades and scuffling of feet.

A cabinet crashed into view around a corner as a Knight Templar splayed out into the four way intersection at the other end of the hall. He quickly collected himself and pushed aside the cabinet that had come with him and disappeared back from where he'd emerged. The backs of several Knights soon rounded the corner and braced themselves against the walls, breathing heavily.

Several Mamluk warriors darted around the corner and continued their assault. The Templars took up arms again, dropping the nearest warriors with concussive impacts from their swords. The Mamluk armor was not up to the grueling abuse the European swords could dish out. Another Templar appeared, running through the remaining Mamluk visible to Johannes and Michael.

"Stay with the Cup," Michael ordered and rushed down the hall toward their Brothers. Another wave of Mamluks appeared around the corner while the three Knights at the end of the hall continued to parry the attacks. Only one of them had a shield and he tried to keep it angled at the hallway corner. Johannes noticed arrows would glance off it once in a while. There were several crossbow bolts sticking through the shield.

As Michael reached the other Templars, the Brother with the shield fell, taken down by a sword edge to the back of the knee. As he crumpled to the ground, Michael swept his sword overhead, knocking chunks of tile loose as it skimmed the ceiling. He brought it down with his whole body, splitting the attacker's helmet and face cleanly in half.

The other two Templars had stopped the portion of the assault directed their way and all three men stepped back against the hallway's corner, waiting for the next wave. Several Mamluks navigated around the bodies of their fallen comrades and took up positions on opposite corners of the hallway intersection. They stared at the Knights but didn't close the distance.

Johannes flicked his eyes back to the Cup. It was safe for the moment. He drew his sword and looked around at the cabinets nearest him. He opened several drawers, looking for anything that might help his situation. He pulled a large paten from one shelf and dumped dried bread from it, hoping it might serve as a make-shift shield.

The Mamluks at the end of the hall numbered 15 by now. They had formed a half circle across the intersection. Finally their reason for waiting became clear as they made room for several archers to set up behind them. Michael and the other two Templars realized and tried to dodge out of the way of the flying bolts. One caught Michael in the shoulder and he spun around, tripping to the ground. The others had been unscathed, but the bolts that missed their marks clattered into cabinets and the walls near Johannes, who ducked back into the Cup's alcove.

He prayed quietly, listening to the noises of smashing furniture and the cries of men being maimed or killed. Michael appeared in the archway of the alcove and shouted, "Destroy it! We are overru—"

A crossbow bolt caught Michael in the throat, cutting off his order. He dropped to his knees, holding his neck and collapsed into the alcove. Johannes started to rush forward to help his Brother but stopped short. His oath was to the Cup. He turned and advanced on the table.

Just before reaching it, he felt a stabbing pain in his back. He couldn't breathe and his right arm went limp. He could hear the scurry of the Mamluks behind him. As he considered the idea that he probably had a bolt sticking out of him, he crashed to one knee and reached out with his left hand. He caught the edge of the fabric covering the table. He felt another bolt pierce him and he collapsed forward, dragging the table contents with him.

The Cup was dragged over the edge of the table by Johannes's grip on the cloth. On his side, with ragged breath, Johannes watched the Cup tip toward him, pouring its contents directly on his face. It was warm. He was blinded briefly by the thick liquid, but heard the cup hit the ground just in front of his nose.

Johannes tasted blood. Was this his own, or from the Cup?

He heard men rushing toward him as he reached for the Cup and caught it by the lip. He prayed for escape. He had visions of returning to the Pope and presenting the only remaining relic from the Mamluk invasion. He felt a sword in his back, twisting, and he snapped back to reality. He must destroy it. He had given his word. There would be no escape and this was likely his last moment. Johannes smashed the Cup to the ground and it shattered. He continued to beat any remaining pieces into the ground with his hand, cutting himself in the process.

A foot stepped on his shoulder, pinning his arm in place. He couldn't move anything anymore and Johannes just stared forward. The shuffling feet and heavy breathing of the warriors around him started to fade into a dull throbbing in his ears. A fragment of the Cup rested against the wall. As his vision retreated, he could make out a portion of the original Aramaic phrase still visible. "Life," Michael had said.

The Mamluks dragged Johannes out of the alcove and into the crowded hallway. There were easily 50 of them standing around between bodies, downed cabinets, and smashed tables. They sheathed swords and worked to clear the hallway of debris. After a few moments of this, they parted, making way for a man dressed in robes. The man entered the alcove and examined the table, then bent to examine the remains of the Cup.

He straightened up violently and started shouting. Johannes couldn't understand him and was surprised he could hear anything at all. The pain in his back had receded and he could flex his fingers again. The flakes of pottery that had been embedded in his left hand sprinkled to the ground. Johannes opened his eyes and saw the back of a Mamluk boot standing in front of his face.

Johannes sat up suddenly, realizing he could breathe. He wiped his face of blood and looked around. One of the Mamluks with him in the hall pointed at him and yelled something, cutting off the robed man's ranting. The warrior standing in front of Johannes spun around and stabbed him in the chest. Johannes coughed blood and glared up at his attacker. The man yanked his sword back out and Johannes felt the pain stop.

He picked up one of the curved Mamluk blades near him and slashed at the man's leg. The man was too surprised to even make a sound and toppled over. Johannes stood and felt a bolt hit him in the gut. He yanked it back out and watched as the wound snapped shut. Several of the Mamluks closest to him stepped back, looking worried.

Johannes screamed and launched himself at the nearest warrior. He felt the frequent sting of stabs and slashes but he kept swinging. Warrior after warrior fell away from him. He had less and less room to swing as he climbed on the bodies of his defeated attackers. They were under foot, draped across broken tables, and pressed against the walls. When there were no more of them, Johannes turned back to the alcove and saw the robed man watching him silently.

The man had managed to reach the forward edge of the alcove, trying to sneak out into the hallway and escape from Johannes. He came to a halt and produced a ceramic globe from his robes. It was about the size of his head, with a wooden stopper in its small mouth. A thin string dangled from the stopper.

Johannes had seen these globes before but he couldn't organize his mind. The robed man leaned back and touched the string to the torch that lit the alcove. The cord sparked and flickered, burning its way toward the top of the globe. Black powder, Johannes remembered dully.

The man rounded the corner into the hallway and continued to back away from Johannes, trying to find stable footing on all the bodies. Johannes hissed at the robed man and launched himself forward, closing the gap. He chopped at the man's hand and the globe fell into the pile of bodies they were balancing on. The man yelled, falling back, and started chanting at Johannes.

Johannes cut the man's throat swiftly and turned back to the globe. The cord had burned down into the stopper. He stepped forward toward it and the world flashed into a catastrophic explosion. Johannes felt the heat and then the crushing weight of dirt and stone from the hall collapsing around him. Everything went dark, but his pain receded again. He couldn't breathe. Each attempt brought dirt and gravel into his lungs. He was caught in a cycle of holding his breath, drowning in a flood of dirt, and back again.

He lost track of time as he tried to dig upward. He could wiggle his fingers, moving his legs from time to time. He tried to transfer dirt from above him, around his body, and down under his feet. It took hours. He found small pockets free of debris as he made progress. After what seemed like an entire day, he reached a solid beam of wood. He could make out light shining in from one end and he'd stopped choking on dirt. He could breathe normally and he relaxed against the beam, shielded from the weight of the church above him. He slept.

Johannes woke in the same position he'd drifted off in: pinned under rubble. It had not been a dream. Or maybe it was? The world was made of stone and wood as far as he could see. He continued to dig out debris along the wooden beam he'd run up against. After another day of slowly shifting stones and dirt, he pushed on a larger stone and it rolled away from him, blasting him with sunlight from the opening it left.

He climbed free from the remains of the collapsed church and faced a surprised group of locals who were working to extract one of the collapsed church walls from the undamaged back half of the building. They stared at him.

2014, Oct 8th, Wednesday

The trip from the airport was relatively short. Rob had gotten a voicemail while they were in the air. It confirmed their visit to Vanda, which was a relief. They didn't need to figure out some other plan to chat with her.

Rob drove quickly, just this side of reckless. Hani wondered if he thought Vanda was going to suddenly die before they got a chance to see her. Regardless, Hani felt perfectly safe. Rob wound between cars on the highway like he was dancing.

The retirement community covered a spacious plot of land. The trees and lawn were well kept, even in the baking sun. Hani'd never really liked the desert and tended toward living places with more seasonality.

Rob parked in a spot marked "visitor" in the second row of cars. The entire first row had been marked as handicapped only. It seemed like a bit of overkill, but then, the residents' average age would probably support the design choice. They left their luggage locked in the Nissan's trunk and made the short trip to the sliding glass doors under a cheerful sign that said, "Welcome home."

The Phoenix Crest Retirement Community's interior looked more like a high-class hotel than a dormitory. Hani wondered if she'd ever spend time in a place like this at the end of her life. She seemed to actually be aging, unlike Rob, so she figured she'd need to consider it eventually. She maybe had another 80 years, but it never hurt to plan ahead.

"Can I help you?" asked the receptionist warmly.

Rob approached and replied, "Hi, thank you, yes. We're here to visit Ms Vanda Engle. I'm Rob McBride and this is Hani Gittel." He waved in Hani's direction as she walked up beside him and smiled. "She's expecting us."

"Certainly. I'll give her a ring. Please make yourself comfortable," the receptionist nodded to the array of couches and chairs in the middle of the foyer as she reached for her phone. Hani found a plush seat to her liking and waited. Rob wandered around the foyer reading the plaques under various photos and paintings.

After a few minutes a man appeared from the hall at the end of the room and approached. He wore a simple white T-shirt and light blue slacks. His name tag said just "Lincoln." He put his hand out to Rob, "Hi, I'm Lincoln. I can show you to Ms Engle's room."

Rob shook his hand and nodded, "Thanks."

Lincoln turned to Hani as she stood up and offered his hand to her as well. Hani took it briefly and smiled. Lincoln turned and headed to the elevator bank just around the corner. They followed him and got on the elevator. He pressed "3" and the doors closed.

"Ms Engle doesn't get a lot of visitors. I'm so glad you could see her," Lincoln said.

"Yeah, we're lucky we were just driving through Phoenix," Hani quickly lied. "I've been wanting to see her for ages."

They reached the third floor and Lincoln led them to 303, letting them in. He announced in a loud voice, "Hello Ms Engle, your guests Rob and Hani are here."

A small voice replied slowly, "Oh thank you, dear. Come on in."

Lincoln held the door for them and then departed, closing the door as he left. Vanda was seated in a small recliner near windows that overlooked the rear courtyard. She adjusted her glasses as Rob and Hani sat down on the couch opposite Vanda's chair. She examined Hani for a moment and said, "Well, you're certainly Hanielle, but you don't look a day over 50. You sure you're not just named after your mother?"

"Hi Miss Schiffer," Hani stumbled over her words. "Sorry, Ms Engle."

"We're all adults now. Call me Vanda, dear," Vanda corrected. "And you? How do you know young Hani here?"

"Hi Ma'am ... Vanda. I'm Rob," Rob ducked his head. "I recently met Hani and we've gotten to know each other quite well. We have a lot in common and part of that may relate to you."

"Oooh," Vanda cooed. "Romance and mystery. I do love a good story. How am I a part of your adventure?"

"Well," Hani started, unsure where to begin. "I'd really like to know if you could help me understand a little more about my childhood. Between my age then and switching to English, I have a hard time remembering details."

"Sprechen Sie Deutsch?" Vanda said carefully, leaning slightly toward Hani.

Hani smiled and replied in English, "It's been a long time, but I still know some German."

"I've forgotten more than I remember," Rob answered in German.

Vanda's eyes lit up at Rob's reply and she cackled happily. "I've kept my practice up. There is a nice couple down the hall that speaks German with me. They came to the States after the second War.

They had a rough time of it back then, but it all worked out. I got lucky, you know, to have my folks move here after the first War."

"I'd wondered how you were so fluent," Hani recalled. "But I'd love to know more about my time at the orphanage. You were my one constant from when I first landed at the airbase right up until high school. None of the other children had the Army checking in with them. What made me special?"

Vanda made a clucking noise and looked out the window again. She stayed silent for several moments. "What do you remember of your piece of ceramic?" She briefly glanced at Rob before settling her eyes back on Hani.

"Before yesterday, I'd mostly put it out of my mind. But after remembering all I'd been put through by the Nazis, a lot of details came back to me. Most notably, I would say, would be the shard's strange ability to, uh, toss people across the room," Hani replied directly.

Vanda watched Rob, but he showed no surprise at Hani's admission. She spoke, "Yes, that was one of its behaviors."

"What can you tell me about it?" Hani asked urgently.

"Well, of anyone, you deserve to know the truth. You forgot about it so quickly as you grew up, we decided not to involve you. Or rather, your involvement was deemed unnecessary and your disinterest in it meant we didn't need to take measures to keep you quiet," Vanda explained.

"What happened to it?" Hani asked.

Vanda ignored her and turned to Rob, "What about you? You here to trick an old woman into giving up National Security Secrets? I doubt my time in prison would last very long." Vanda chuckled fitfully under her breath.

"No Ma'am," Rob answered, "I'm here to learn the same truth as Hani."

Vanda shifted back to Hani, "You sure you want this? We don't need to involve anyone new in this curse."

Rob replied before Hani could answer, "Ms Engle, I made an oath to protect the world from this object, and I thought I'd already succeeded. I am here to finish the job."

Hani twisted to face Rob. She hadn't really considered what they were going to do with the shard once they got it. She had mostly assumed it wasn't going to be possible for them to even find it in the first place. "You want to destroy it?"

Vanda's eyes bounced back and forth between Rob and Hani.

Rob said, "Yes. Look at what the Nazis did with it. Look what it did to both of us. What happens when evil wields it? I vowed to either protect it from being stolen or destroy it. I thought I had destroyed it, but now I know it's been found. Someone literally dug it up."

Vanda's eyes had fallen to Rob and stayed fixed on him.

"Okay, sure. No objections from me," Hani resolved, turning back to Vanda.

"Hanielle, you aged slowly. We figured that out, but it didn't seem to effect you too terribly, so we never confronted you with it," Vanda said without looking away from Rob. "You, though. Rob, is it? How old are you?"

Without flinching, Rob said, "729."

Vanda closed her eyes, eased back in her chair, and sighed. "The Templar."

Hani's eyebrows shot up and Rob leaned forward slightly.

Vanda opened her eyes again and focused on Rob. "I always said you must still be around. They told me it was just hysterical religious writings about the Sack of the Reliquary and the Undying Knight. But I was convinced. Were you the Golem of Passchendaele?"

Rob frowned, "The what?"

"There was a story of a Golem, a warrior made of living mud, that became an unstoppable force in the trenches of Passchendaele. Bullets would pass through it, leaving it untouched. Explosions would only slow it down as the mud would recollect from the trench walls and stand up again, killing every German that was unlucky enough to cross its path."

"It was very wet in the trenches that day, yes, but I'm not made of mud," Rob replied. "I've never heard that title before, but I figured the men that followed in my wake couldn't have stayed silent like I asked them."

"Ever burned as a witch?" Vanda continued.

"Yes," Rob admitted.

"I figured they couldn't have all been just regular people," Vanda said. "Oh, you have no idea how satisfying this is."

"Vanda," Hani interrupted, "We really need to know about the shard. Where is it?"

Vanda straightened up again and said, "Nevada. First they experimented with it at the airbase in Massachusetts, but it proved quite dangerous. After several injuries, they shipped it to a base in Nevada. It was ignored for several decades, but a few years ago a professor came to visit me and wanted to know more about it. He said he wanted to harness its energy amplification properties for one of the anti-ICBM projects the government had cooked up."

"Do you remember his name?" Rob asked.

"Tillinghast," Vanda recalled. "Last I heard, he was still chipping away at it. I don't remember what the project is called anymore, though. It was classified to start with and I know it got renamed a few times."

"Do you remember his first name?" Hani tag-teamed.

"Oh, what did they call him? Ford? It was Clifford or Crawford, or something like that. I only met him a few times," Vanda said.

"Thank you so much Vanda, this has been extremely helpful," Hani said.

"Absolutely, dear. I always felt so bad that we were never able to tell you the truth about the object. You were just a child, though," Vanda admitted.

"That's fine, Vanda, I understand," Hani said, getting up to hug her ancient friend.

"Thank you," Rob said.

Vanda smiled. "Rob, if you ever figure out how to pass on your little death-cheating trick, please keep me in mind. I don't think I've got much road left, but I'd like more."

"You have my word, Ms Engle," Rob promised. "Though I must say, I have spent quite a bit of time studying my condition and, so far, it seems entirely untransferable."

Vanda took Rob's outstretched hand with both of hers, "Thank you. Please visit again. I want to know how this story ends."

Hani and Rob let themselves out of Vanda's room and found their way back down to the parking lot. In the car, Rob browsed through hotel listings on his phone looking for one near the airport. Hani booted her computer again to see if she could locate this Tillinghast.

2014, Oct 9th, Thursday

Tillinghast looked up from his console at the arcs of energy surrounding the Amplifier in a glowing orb. It rotated slowly in the orb, just above a pedestal on the story-high platform at the center of the large chamber. The readings were amazing.

Landon leaned over, "Does that really say what I think it does? The jump in energy output this morning has radically passed our projections."

"This is what I've always known would be possible," Tillinghast said proudly. "We've finally gotten a stable rift."

They watched the small, dark, almond-shaped hole hovering at waist height behind the Amplifier's orb, above the center of the platform.

Tillinghast stood up and turned to the room of technicians seated in concentric half-circle rows of consoles behind him, filling the Amplification Chamber. "Everyone!" His voice echoed through the circular concrete chamber.

A few people emerged from equipment cages at the back of the room. The guard standing next to the only exit, a giant metal roll-up door, stood up straighter. Tillinghast's eyes tracked across the two stretches of second story windows that overlooked the chamber on either side of the roll-up door. Several people were looking down from them into the chamber, their faces reflecting the dim glow of their control stations.

"With your help, I have ushered in a new era of energy independence!" he bellowed.

Clapping erupted around him and he smiled widely. "With this rift, there is no limit to the energy we can harness. This will be the ultimate renewable!"

Landon remained focused on his console.

Tillinghast continued as the clapping started to die down, "Alright, everyone, let's get back to work. It's time for Phase 4."

"Doctor," Landon touched Tillinghast's arm lightly. "How is this possible? You didn't raise the reactor output. The Amplifier has been spontaneously improving the focusing efficiency for the past few hours. We didn't adjust anything."

"None of that matters, Landon." Tillinghast sat back down, bouncing slightly in his chair. He let the satisfaction of his success wash over him.

"I don't know what's changed," Landon mused.

Tillinghast ignored him. "We need to turn up the reactors."

"But we haven't tested that range," Landon said, confused.

"Can't you hear it?" Tillinghast demanded. "It's crying out for our attention. We have to take this all the way."

"I—" Landon cut himself short. "Yes. I'll monitor from the reactor controls upstairs."

"What? No, stay here. I need you watching the resonance. The techs up there are perfectly capable of running the reactors." Tillinghast studied the windows again for a moment.

"Yes, Doctor," Landon intoned.

Tillinghast typed furiously into his console, and the chamber started to fill with a low hum. The hole in the air above the platform inflated slightly.

"Did you see that?" Tillinghast nudged Landon. "It's never been that large before!"

"We should focus it higher in the chamber. I'm not sure what'll happen if it intersects the platform," Landon cautioned.

"Not yet. Is the energy signature matching our projections?"

"The readings don't make any sense," Landon said, rechecking his screens. He looked back up at the rift, frowning.

"I'm taking the reactors to full output," Tillinghast said, mostly to himself.

Landon turned sharply to face Tillinghast. "Wait, no, we need to clear the chamber for full output! The shielding between the reactor rooms and here isn't sufficient for a sustained run."

Tillinghast didn't acknowledge him and finished typing in the last of the commands. As the hum grew, the arcs of energy coming into the orb around the Amplifier crackled loudly, and the smell of ozone wafted through the chamber. The rip grew to the width of a beach ball. The interior seemed to flicker.

"Can you hear that?" Tillinghast got up from his console and walked into the wide aisle that stretched from the platform to the roll-up doors. He stepped forward and past the row of consoles, making his way around the platform, toward one of the two ladders on either side that lead to the top.

Landon watched Tillinghast. "All I hear is the Amplifier." Before Landon could figure out what was happening, Tillinghast had scaled the ladder and was up on the platform, striding towards the growing hole in the air.

Landon jumped up from his chair, "Doctor! What are you doing?!"

The guard stationed at the roll-up doors had started jogging down the aisle toward the platform. Several of the other technicians had stood up, looking as puzzled as Landon.

"At least check your dosimeter!" Landon shouted as he checked his own. It showed elevated radiation levels, though nothing near fatal yet. But he wasn't standing on the pedestal.

Tillinghast stared into the rift, ignoring the commotion growing down on the chamber floor. The tear was wide enough now that he could see clearly into it. It led somewhere else, as they had measured. It looked like a shimmering field of stars, like he was looking through a porthole on a clear night. He walked around it and the perspective through the tear shifted with him. He really was looking through a rip into another universe.

He tuned out Landon's shouting. Something about not touching it. It seemed lonely. He reached out and caressed the boundary layer between the worlds. It felt cold as he skimmed his fingertips across the surface. He pulled back and studied his fingers. They looked fine. In fact, they felt great. He felt great. It was so clear now.

Landon's eyes were wide as he quickly turned back to his console. He started typing desperately, trying to shut down the reactors. He had been locked out.

Tillinghast turned to look down towards the room of alarmed scientists. His smile grew. "More!"

Unable to gain reactor control, Landon tried to move the rift up away from Tillinghast's grasp. He still had access to focus controls. After a few adjustments, the rift bobbed up well out of Tillinghast's reach.

Tillinghast started screaming as the rift floated up to its new position above his head. He jumped fruitlessly, trying to touch it again. He scanned the chamber. His eyes flicked up, settling on the crane above the platform on the high ceiling. The crane gantry access steps zigzagged up the back wall, and he started to move towards the ladder on the opposite side of the platform.

The guard cleared the top of the ladder and stood on the platform with Tillinghast, blocking his way down to the gantry steps. He gestured with one hand, demanding Tillinghast vacate the platform. With his other hand, the guard snapped open the clasp on his holster.

Tillinghast's scream shifted into laughter.

Exploration

Rob parked at the side of the Nevada road and got out. Hani followed suit and they hiked up the ridge. At the crest, they stayed low, getting on their hands and knees. They looked south into the valley below and studied the military installation Hani had found after locating Crawford Tillinghast. It was morning, but the floodlights were still on, illuminating the entire length of the razor-wire-topped chain link fence. A single road approached the base and passed by a guard house before crossing through a rolling gate. Inside, the road branched out several times. There were seven buildings of varying sizes inside the confines of the fence. They were mostly configured close together at the north end of the base.

The single gate was at the center of the northern span of the fence line. To the south, and slightly west, was what looked like a dormitory. There were a few satellite TV dishes sticking out at various points along the very regular window placements and small balconies. The building south of the housing looked like it belonged in an office park with its wide dark windows. To the east of the entry road was a large garage with several Humvees parked out front. South of the garage was what looked like a cross between a barn and an aircraft hangar. Between the office building and the hangar, at the center of the entire installation, was a much smaller building with no windows that appeared to exist mostly to hold up a giant air conditioning unit. The remaining two buildings were the only structures in the entire southern half of the base. They were identical in appearance and placed opposite each other in the two southern corners of the base. Each looked like a small nuclear cooling tower with no windows and no doors. They both produced a small trickle of steam.

"Office, hangar, or apartments?" Hani asked, handing the binoculars back to Rob.

"Well, we have no idea where the shard might be, even if it is here. I feel like we should try to avoid people as much as possible, at least initially. Let's see if there's much activity during the day, but I think the hangar would be the best place to start. Maybe it's just locked up in there and we can drift right back out without anyone knowing what's happening," Rob suggested.

"I guess so. I was thinking we'd be better off finding this Tillinghast so we could ask him—" Hani was interrupted by a small tremor.

Rob frowned and put the binoculars to his face. A set of red lights had turned on above the door on the center building. As he watched, the doors opened and several people in lab coats burst out, followed by several men in uniforms. A few tripped in their rush to get through the door and fell to the ground. Others helped them up and then continued running. They were met by other people that had left the office building, and several of the Humvees were departing the garage. Everyone looked quite disorganized.

"I changed my mind," Hani said. "I think we should go to that central building first."

Rob lowered the binoculars, "Agreed. Should we wait for night fall?"

"No," Hani said confidently. "If they're going to notice us during the day, they're going to be equipped to see us at night too. I think we should go now ... they're clearly confused. Let's get in there and learn whatever we can."

"Okay, let's get moving," Rob declared. They stood up and climbed over the crest. It was a quick hike down the ridge into the valley. They'd circled east to approach the southeastern corner of the fence line. During the 20 minutes it took them, the commotion in the base appeared to have subsided.

"This cooling tower looked smaller from up there," Hani observed. She put out her hand for Rob. He took it. Hani said, "Okay, get close to the fence."

Rob followed Hani's lead and got within licking distance of the fence. He felt her grip tighten slightly on his hand and then he was suddenly a foot and a half closer to the cooling tower with no fence in sight. He felt Hani drop his hand and he looked behind himself. The fence was almost touching his heel. "That is such a strange sensation. It feels like nothing at all, but I'm suddenly somewhere else."

Hani closed her eyes for a moment and then opened them, straighting up slightly. "Well, I'm still getting used to doing this with more than just me. Glad it's still working, though."

Rob jogged up to the cooling tower and walked around to the corner of the structure. He crouched down and brought up the binoculars again. He scanned the gravel and sand between them and the central building. He couldn't see anyone else at the moment. Everyone had retreated into either the office or the apartments while they had made their way down the ridge. Excepting the now empty Humvees that had been moved to block the northern gate, nothing else seemed to have visibly changed.

Rob and Hani jogged across the open field, trying to use the hangar to block any line of sight from the apartments. The central building partially blocked anyone that might look out their office windows. Rob was worried about the garage, though, since they were just out in the open from that direction. So far, so good. No surprises.

They rounded the central building. On the north side, it had a large roll-up door with a set of double doors next to it. The red lights were still on and the air conditioning was running steadily. Rob tried one of the doors. It was unlocked. "Ladies first," he offered.

Hani curtsied and then trotted inside with Rob following closely behind. They were in a large white room with a single cargo elevator in the center. On either side of the elevator were cooling pipes and what seemed to be high voltage power conditioning equipment. A red light, matching the ones outside, was flashing above the elevator doors.

"Did you ever meet Nikola Tesla?" Hani asked, eying the electrical gear.

"Hmm? No, I learned about him too late," Rob said as they approached the elevator. He pressed the single button available: down. The elevator dinged cheerfully and the huge doors opened. An entire tank could have fit in the elevator.

"Ah, bummer. He was quite remarkable. I'd always wished I could have talked with him just for a few minutes," Hani said as they stepped inside.

With very little choice again, Rob selected "B" and the elevator doors closed. Several minutes later when the doors opened again, they were greeted by a tall, white corridor. That same tank from the elevator could have comfortably navigated forward here.

"This goes south, doesn't it?" Hani confirmed.

"Yeah," Rob agreed. "What the hell is this place?"

They jogged down the hall covering the short distance to a huge set of steel doors that just had the word "BLAST" stenciled across them. There were no buttons, no intercoms, no key holes. As they pondered this situation, Rob felt the small tremor again, this time a bit stronger. Just before the shaking stopped, he noticed Hani blink out of existence for a half second, accompanied by the now familiar air displacement popping.

"Did I—" Hani started to ask.

"Yes." Rob said. "You just vanished. Involuntary?"

"Yeah," Hani said, looking around.

"Well that can't be good ... Regardless, I guess we go through this," Rob said, pointing at the blast doors.

Hani snagged Rob's hand and closed her eyes slowly as they stepped forward almost pressing against the doors. An instant later for Rob the doors were behind them, with a bit more hallway ahead. Hani let out a long breath, "Those things were really thick."

"How long were we gone?" Rob asked.

"Well, I think I'm learning how to drift faster, but I'd guess that took about 4 hours," Hani estimated.

"What are they trying to keep in?" Rob wondered, looking back at the blast doors.

A few steps forward from this side of the doors the hallway branched off in opposite directions, curving to the east and west. Ahead was a short section of hallway that ended in a ramp leading down to what appeared to be a large tank-width steel roll-up door. On either side before the ramp were doors that led into window-lined control rooms. Through the control room windows on the right, Rob could see a man feverishly running between computer stations. While they watched, he'd sometimes pause briefly, looking through a further set of windows that overlooked whatever was on the other side of roll-up doors, before continuing his stereotypy.

"Let's ask him," Hani suggested.

Landon

Hani tried the control room door. It was unlocked, so they just walked through it like they belonged. The technician looked up, surprised. "Oh, uh, who are you?" was all he managed, without taking this hands off his currently chosen keyboard.

"I'm Hani. This is Rob. We're looking for Crawford Tillinghast. Have you seen him?" Hani inquired directly.

"What? Yeah, of course. He's down in the Amplification Chamber," he nodded over his shoulder toward the wall of windows overlooking the area beyond the roll-up door. "You really shouldn't be here."

"What's happening?" Hani asked. They'd walked closer to the technician, around various control stations, and had to push in office chairs that had been scattered hastily in the aisles. His badge read "Landon Sibley."

Landon stopped typing for a moment and studied them. "Who are you? I've never seen you before."

"We were sent to check on things here," Hani attempted.

"We didn't evacuate with the others," Rob tried to come up with some supporting statements for this bluff.

"Well, you're just as dead as me, I guess," Landon's feverish movements started to calm down a bit as he moved down a few workstations and starting typing again.

"How so?" Hani frowned.

"The reactors are surging," Landon explained. "We'd never gotten this far before. This morning the Amplifier's efficiency went through the roof. No clue why. Dr Tillinghast didn't care to know why and just cranked the reactors up to full. That's when we started getting the feedback pulses. The energy output has been staggering, but now we can't shut it down. When the radiation surges got too high, the alarms went off and everyone cleared out. I stayed because I thought I could trick the relays into shutting down. But that didn't work and, when the next surge hit, the blast doors slammed shut."

"Radiation surges?" Rob repeated.

"Yeah, the reactors keep going into overdrive. The time between surges has been getting shorter and shorter. I had hoped to increase it so the blast door fail-safes would disengage, but since we keep releasing more radiation and doing it more frequently, I don't see a way to get out of here. It doesn't matter for us now, though," Landon half-heartedly yanked on his badge, facing it toward them.

Hani noticed a large red dot at the bottom of the badge now.

Landon continued, "The dosimeter says I'm dead already. It's just a matter of my body shutting down now. In the meantime, I'm going to keep trying to find a way to stop this thing. If I don't, we're all dead."

Rob considered all the people they'd seen rushing out of here, "Can you stall for time? It looked like everyone else was evacuating with serious dedication."

"Oh, no, I meant 'all' very literally," Landon explained calmly. "Dr Tillinghast has ripped a hole in our universe and he seems dedicated to widening it. If I can't find a way to disengage the reactors before he has a stable energy feedback through the inter-dimensional rift, I'm pretty sure our little facility here will single-handedly destroy the planet. Maybe even the whole solar system. I really don't know, but the energy readings through the rift are off the charts."

Rob and Hani studied Landon carefully.

"Destroy ... the planet?" Rob managed.

"Right. That's bad." Hani said slowly.

Landon started laughing, but managed to choke it under control. "Here I thought we'd finally unlocked the Amplifier's secrets and we'd get unlimited free energy for the planet. I guess the 'unlimited' part really meant 'uncontrollable.'"

"There must be a way to stop this," Rob demanded.

"If so, we're running out of time. Each surge happens more quickly than the last and when there's no delay left between them, I think the rift will be self-sustaining. Right now, both reactors are needed to keep the rift open. They're being used to widen the tear. Once the rift is large enough, its own power output will be sufficient to keep things moving. I've been trying to shut the reactors down from here, but Tillinghast has stayed one step ahead of me," Landon detailed.

"So we need to knock out both reactors," Rob repeated. "Are they under the cooling towers?"

"Yes, yes. Or we can remove the Amplifier from the circuit," Landon said.

"The amplifier?" Hani questioned.

"Yeah, the artifact. It's in there with Tillinghast," Landon explained, frustrated.

"A small piece of ceramic?" Hani asked.

"Yes, the Amplifier," Landon repeated. "Look, I don't know who you people are, but I've got to stop this and I need to concentrate."

Rob cleared his throat, "We can help."

"Oh really? You can get through the six foot thick blast doors around the reactors? Or walk into the Amplification Chamber with Tillinghast? That lunatic is armed! Don't you think that's the first thing I tried? He almost shot me. I think he killed the guard when he took his gun." Landon thrust an arm at the windows, pointing, "It's a good thing this plexiglass is so damn strong. If not, I think Tillinghast would have tried to shoot me from down there too. He's gone crazy, but he's still smart."

"I can get through the blast doors," Hani said flatly.

"They can't be opened! They slammed shut with the first radiation surge!" Landon exclaimed, breathlessly.

"And I can stop Tillinghast," Rob said.

"Well then you guys go do it!" Landon yelled, nearly crazed himself, waving them away from his consoles.

Tillinghast

Rob and Hani returned to the main hallway that led back to the reactor access hallways and forward to the Amplification Chamber ramp and roll-up door.

"Alright, I'll go take care of the shard. You'll go shut down a reactor?" Rob confirmed.

"Yeah, it sounded like we needed to get two out of three of these things stopped to keep the rift from going stable. I've gotten faster, but it'll still take me a couple hours to get through the other blast—", Hani was interrupted as she blinked out of existence.

Rob felt a mild tingling sensation and then it was gone.

Hani reappeared, "—doors." Hani frowned.

"I think that was another radiation surge," Rob guessed. "You keep vanishing when they happen. I felt it this time ... almost like a hot breeze."

"Yeah, this sucks. If those get close enough together to be ongoing, I'm going to end up displaced until you shut down the amplifier," Hani worried.

"Yeah, let's get moving. If Landon survives, maybe he can help me get the blast doors open again if I can subdue Tillinghast," Rob said.

"Okay, see you on the other side," Hani waved and started running back the way they'd come and then turned left down the western reactor hall, disappearing around the corner.

Rob jogged down the ramp to the roll-up door. To the side on the right wall there was a small control panel. Rob pressed the clearly marked "up" button and the door shivered. It started to rise, producing a horrible shrieking of metal on metal. This was not going to be a stealthy approach, but he assumed that wasn't required.

The Amplification Chamber was the size of a high school gymnasium, only circular. Sections of the chamber wall nearest the entrance were actually recessed rooms, separated from the chamber by metal mesh walls and punctuated at their ends with doors made from the same metal mesh. The rooms were filled with shop machinery, computer racks, and other gear that Rob couldn't easily identify. Within the chamber, the next ring forward, were console stations. About half the stations had things flickering across their monitors and their companion desk chairs were scattered randomly. A few lay on their side.

At the center of the room was a metal platform. Two huge cables, each as big around as a truck, snaked in from opposite walls and joined machinery under the platform. At the near edge of the platform was a pedestal with a glowing orb above it. The orb seemed to be drawing power through a steady maelstrom of lightning coming up from under the platform. Something small rotated lazily in the middle of the arcing orb. Rob assumed this was the shard. Beyond the pedestal at the center of the platform and floating about 20 feet up, seemingly projected by the orb, was a person-high rip in the air.

Rob found the tear hard to see. Looking at it required focusing his eyes out much further than even the far wall of the chamber. As it drew waves of energy in from the artifact-powered orb, he could make out stars, as if he were looking at a sliver of the night sky within this rip in reality. Lights twinkled from the depths, but none of them were white. He saw shades of red, green, yellow, violet, and blue. They felt like eyes, boring into him. He was being watched from the other side, from far beyond.

Rob was so stunned by the sight of the tear that he hadn't initially registered the body of the guard laying halfway down the aisle that lead between the roll-up door and the platform. Nor did he notice Tillinghast until a gunshot rang out and Rob's attention was snapped back by the searing pain in his shoulder. He felt his humerus knitting itself back together after being splintered by a bullet.

Tillinghast was walking down a series of steps attached to a gantry crane that fit snuggly across the ceiling of the chamber. The crane hook hung limply above the rip. Tillinghast's gun smoked as he jumped down the last few steps and straightened up. "Get out!" he yelled.

"Sorry, I've got to get my shard back," Rob apologized while he kept moving.

"Heretic! Meddler!" Tillinghast yelled, raising the gun again as he broke into a run toward Rob.

Rob managed to dodge a few shots, but took two to the chest. He caught his breath again and straightened back up as the bullets were spat out of this body to the floor.

"No one can stop the Awakening! I have heard their calls! Their will is undeniable! The Great Ones will devour us in everlasting ecstasy!" Tillinghast diverted to the guard's body.

Rob continued his approach. Just a few more yards and Rob would be on top of him. He wasn't sure how to stop the shard, but figured a office chair through the orb would probably knock it out of place. Beyond that, borrowing Tillinghast's gun and just shooting the platform machinery seemed reasonable. Both Landon and Tillinghast had absorbed beyond lethal levels of radiation at this point, so any explosion here wouldn't change their fates. Rob and Hani would be fine. He might have to wait a while for Hani to drift to the surface, but it should be over quickly.

Tillinghast bent down and pulled something from the guard's belt. Before Rob could discern its purpose, Tillinghast had fired. Pain seared across Rob's chest and he dropped to his knees. He was paralyzed. Before he passed out, he understood what the pair of wires leading from the new weapon to his chest meant: a Taser.

Rob's eyes fluttered open a moment later to find Tillinghast bent over him with a frown. Before Rob could sweep the Taser barbs from his shirt, he got hit again with a jolt of electricity.

"They send a demon to stop me!" Tillinghast screamed to no one in particular. "But even this demon has a weakness. Just like all the others!"

Rob tried to keep his head clear, but kept passing out as Tillinghast dragged him backward away from the platform between shocks.

Tillinghast continued to rant as he hauled Rob into one of the machinery rooms along the side of the chamber. "I know what you're thinking," Tillinghast said in a deadpan. "'Did he zap me six times or only five?' Well to tell you the truth," he started giggling and hit Rob with the Taser again, "in all this excitement I kinda lost track myself. But being this is a—" Tillinghast looked at the side of the Taser as Rob tried to collect his thoughts long enough to resist. "—X26P Taser, the most powerful conducted electrical weapon in the world, and would zap your head clean off, you've gotta ask yourself one question."

Rob felt something wrapping around his wrist and heard it ratcheting closed. Before he could tug his hand away, Tillinghast paralyzed him again.

"'Do I feel lucky?'" Tillinghast closed the other half of the pair of handcuffs around Rob's other wrist, "Well, do ya, punk?" He doubled over with laughter as Rob's head finally cleared long enough to understand what was happening.

Rob had been handcuffed around some kind of cooling pipe that ran through the back of the machine room. Tillinghast was getting back up, wiping tears from his eyes. He'd dropped the Taser and wandered out of the room.

"You're amazing," he said over his shoulder to Rob. "I've never seen anything like that. But you're just another mystery that I'll uncover at the end of this. I will understand everything. This universe and the next will be my playground." He slammed the metal mesh door shut, locking it.

Rob struggled against the handcuffs with no luck. He kicked at the cooling pipe, but it didn't budge. It was probably rated for way higher pressures than he could exert.

"Just a few more minutes," Tillinghast's voice trailed away as he retreated to the platform.

Rob tried yanking at his hands with all his might, trying to cut into his wrists with the edge of the handcuffs, but his skin just regrew, shoving its way under the cuffs. He relaxed and considered his options for escape. Tillinghast had put the cuffs on quite tight. He'd seen escape artists dislocate their thumbs to get out of these things.

Rob took a few breaths and then levered his left arm down onto his right thumb just at the base of his wrist. It hurt like hell, but he persisted. He bounced all of his weight down sharply and felt the joint dislocate and then immediately bind itself together again, shoving the cuffs back up his wrist where they'd started.

Through the wire mesh of his cage, he could see Tillinghast

climbing up to the platform. Tillinghast checked his watch briefly and then threw his arms above his head like he was being asked to surrender. There was a shift in the air. A wind picked up and there was a popping crack as the tear suddenly widened substantially. Rob could hear fragments of Tillinghast chanting something over the racket of the lightning feeding the orb. A deep droning started and Tillinghast lowered one arm, keeping his right hand up, fingers outstretched toward the rift.

From the edges of the rip, tendrils of light wiggled out. They threaded their way through the air like electrified spilled liquid. They undulated in place, growing out and touching down on Tillinghast's palm. On contact, a surge of energy poured through the tendrils and enveloped his body. He shrieked in delight as he absorbed the pulses.

He raised his left hand again and the energy shot from him into the center of the rift. This new flood of power appeared to widen the rift further, surging in small increments.

Rob was paralyzed again, this time by fear. This was what Landon must have meant. It was partially self-sustaining now: the energy from the rift was being redirected by Tillinghast back into further widening the tear, which gave him even more energy than the reactors were providing to add into the feedback loop.

The top seam of the tear had reached the ceiling. Chunks of concrete were ripped from the ceiling and drifted away into the space on the other side. Rob hoped Hani was able to knock out both reactors before Tillinghast was able to entirely sustain the rift growth. Rob tried not to think about how large this was going to get.

Timing

Hani raced down the bare corridor. Based on the layout she'd seen above and the distance she'd run already, these reactors were clearly what the cooling towers above ground were tied to, confirming Landon's description of her goal. As she came to a stop in front of the western reactor's blast doors, Hani felt the world flicker gray again as another radiation surge pulsed through the complex. If these blast doors were actually providing shielding, those surges were serious business on the other side.

She took a few steps back and then took a running start, trying to transfer her kinetic energy into a state of mind. A fast state of mind. She blinked out of time and tried to push herself forward at the same speed she'd managed while sprinting. The metal of the doors absorbed her and she felt herself sliding forward through it rapidly. Sprint, sprint, she held on to the sensation of the motion.

Hani emerged from the doors and stumbled into the reactor control room, just managing to keep her feet under her. How long had that been? Maybe 30 seconds? That was way faster.

The room was filled with the bleating of alarms. To her left was a long curving wall with a flashlight, first aid kit, and a fire ax hanging from pegs. The world blinked gray involuntarily again and Hani looked right to see a bank of warning lights start flashing aggressively.

Looking forward, she felt like she was on a Star Trek set. The room opened up into a three story high chamber. From floor to ceiling at the center of the room was what looked, at first, like a grain silo. The metal column had large windows cut in its sides, showing some kind of glowing yellow substance swirling frenetically through its full height. On the wall to the right with the lights were banks of more lights, controls, and several computer stations.

She surveyed the consoles. Most showed pegged gauges and red-lettered warnings. There did not seem to be an obvious "off" button anywhere. She'd kind of hoped for giant red emergency stop button like you find on heavy machinery. She considered her options and the world flickered gray again. The surges were getting way too close together.

Remembering the cooling towers again, Hani ran around to the other side of the towering reactor column. Here pipes of various shapes, sizes, and colors all fed in from the ceiling, down the back wall and curved to attach at the base of the column. Four of the larger pipes were blue and were painted with arrows pointing toward the column. They seemed to match four others that were red with arrows pointing away and up toward the ceiling.

The world flicked gray, maybe for an instant longer. No time for finesse. She ran back around the plasma silo and yanked the fire ax off the wall. She tried to grasp what building safety code might have dictated its inclusion in the reactor floor plan. "Section 5: Electrical Interference. Category 13: Human emotional response. In case of frustrating computer error, an ax must be within 40 feet for use as a computer attitude readjustment tool. Insert ax in monitor. Repeat until frustration abates." Hani read out her imagined building code as she ran back across the room to the rear of the reactor column.

She climbed up on the pipes as high as she could get while still being able to reach the blue cooling pipes below her. As she swung the ax overhead, she blinked away and back again. She noted she'd taken the ax with her. She must have felt quite attached to it. Refocusing, she continued her swing and thunked through insulation around the cooling pipe. She repeated her efforts, jarring her arms with each metal against metal strike.

On the sixth swing, the pipe cracked open and a neon green liquid sprayed out. She covered her face, but didn't disappear. She figured it must not have been particularly poisonous. After a moment, the pipe violently split totally open and the coolant gushed out in huge arcing rush, covering the floor of the reactor chamber. She felt the world flicker again and shifted her position to start on the next pipe. She angled her hits to try to maximize impact on bottom tip of the ax blade. Three strikes in and the second pipe burst open.

As Hani continued her assault on the defenseless coolant pipes, she heard a new alarm start going off. This one was much deeper, with a longer blast between moments of silence, like what she imagined a tractor trailer horn would sound like under water. Her hands were aching. She paused to adjust her grip and she flickered out of the world again.

Gritting her teeth, she timed her strikes to the new thunderous alarm throbs. The third pipe ruptured after the fourth hit. The floor was almost two feet deep in escaped coolant. She moved again, getting an angle on the last pipe. A radiation surge interrupted her concentration on the upswing and she almost dropped the ax. She choked up on her grip and swung again. She'd improved her technique with practice it seemed, since the second strike popped the fourth pipe wide open.

She slid and climbed her way down the pipes and sloshed across the chamber to the consoles, dropping the ax on the way. Twice she'd flickered out of time. Displacing while standing in three feet of liquid did weird things. She left huge waves each time she returned. She estimated she had about 10 seconds between surges now and the gap was shrinking quickly.

The middle monitor now simply said "EVACUATE." As a matter of full disclosure, it also helpfully included some reasoning about this declaration in the form of a count-down after the phrase "core over-temperature condition." It read just under 4 minutes. She blinked away and splashed back into the room. She wasn't going to have enough time to get through the blast door.

Hani bolted for the door. Blink, splash, splash, blink, splash, blink, blink. She was arms-length from the etching that said "BLAST." She looked over her shoulder at the plasma column which had started hissing ominously. The world went gray and stayed that way. The radiation from the reactor was now leaking without abatement. She counted the minutes down, hoping Rob had gotten the shard away from Tillinghast. Three, one-thousand. Two, one-thousand. One, one-thousand.

At the familiar fast-forward speeds, Hani watched the reactor chamber explode in a searing white flash. It took the ceiling clear off the room in a giant upward cone. Several stories above her, she could see the Nevada sky though the rapidly clearing smoke. As the sun set, she saw to her left some kind of giant black dome growing up out of the ground, consuming everything it touched. The edges looked like static, which at first was all that differentiated it from Nevada's night sky. The stars in the growing dome seemed just as distant, but they were packed closer together and multicolored.

After a few seconds, the wall to her left collapsed into the rapidly growing void of the dome. The static at the edges looked more like tentacles now. She felt the stars nearest to her turn, as if looking in her direction.

Collapse

Rob sat slumped at the back of the machine room, watching the giant sphere growing, eating the back wall of the chamber. He'd given up trying to escape. Even his attempts to bite through his wrist had failed. His mouth remained coppery from his own blood.

Whatever was on the other side of that rift looked like it was going to make his time in the Atlantic look like a brisk walk in the park. He closed his eyes and tried to prepare himself for the end of the world. A slow parade of faces wandered across his thoughts. Hani, his new friend, delighted at the success of controlling impossible abilities. She drifted away, giving way to Marie and the look on her face while they watched the moving pictures in Paris. He thought of the mud-covered men from his World War troop as they clambered into a stolen German tank. A quick glimpse of his Atlantic-crossing shipmates as they drank over dinner, laughing and spilling rum on each other. He remembered the early times sharing meals with his hosts in Olevia, before they turned on him. He quickly pushed them from his mind and his fellow Templars filled the void. They had trained together, sharing stories of their homes.

He thought of his parents. It was so very long ago. There were huge sections of multiple centuries that he couldn't remember clearly, but he could still make out his mother and father. His father had gone mostly bald before Rob had become a squire for the Church. Rob smiled to himself, wondering what his father would have done for the ability to grow his hair out at will. Rob frowned. What would his father have made of his little boy, Johannes, bound to a wall while a mad-man toiled to destroy their world?

In sudden realization, Rob's eyes snapped open. He focused on Tillinghast, who was still cackling and chanting on the platform, acting as some infernal conduit for the energies that were being unleashed by the rift. Rob lowered his gaze to his arms and tried to remember what it felt like to be a boy. He'd been skinny, even if he was strong from helping in the fields. He shifted his gaze to his chest, his legs, feet. This was his body. But it was from when he'd fallen in the reliquary below the church. The clothes were from now. He bought these pants from a shop down the street from his condo. This body was no different from clothes.

He concentrated, shedding himself of the bulk he'd gained as a Templar, the height he'd gained when he was 15. He felt his shirt beginning to pool around his neck and he kept retracting, pulling his body back to a state much younger, but still himself. His perspective on the room had shifted now that he was so much smaller. The handcuffs slid from his 12 year old boy wrists and he stood, freed from the shackles. Tillinghast still had his back to Johannes.

Johannes? His thinking was a bit muddled from this alteration. He was a bit dizzy and caught himself on the pipes, sitting back down quickly. He focused again on where he was. He had to stop Tillinghast. He concentrated again on his self-image. He needed to be full-grown. He needed the muscle and the height. His body size expanded again, bulking back up to its regular proportions. He adjusted his shirt and put his shoes back on quickly, keeping an eye on Tillinghast.

He picked up the Taser that Tillinghast has discarded. The battery level was low, so he pitched it back into the corner of the room. Not even bothering to try the knob, Rob kicked open the wire mesh cage door and started winding his way through the console aisle. He wasn't sure what was going to be the best way to handle Tillinghast. The man was channeling untold energies from another universe. Rob wasn't looking forward to what might be a rift-powered human Taser. Rob picked up the last chair in the aisle as he turned to the platform. Maybe the shard could be disrupted instead.

Rob brought the chair over his head, preparing to toss it at the shard from where he was standing below the platform. Before he could finish his wind-up, there was a thundering explosion that shook the chamber. The wall to the right buckled inward several feet, with furrows running from floor to ceiling. Chunks of concrete fell, pulverizing the consoles and desks below the cracking wall.

The machinery under the platform sputtered and all of the lightning feeding the right half of the pedestal abruptly stopped. Rob grinned slightly. Hani certainly had a flare for sabotage. The rift shivered and slowed its expansion, but didn't stop. Tillinghast snarled at the wall, but still hadn't noticed Rob, instead returning his attention to feeding energy back into the rift.

Rob tossed the chair at the pedestal. As the chair arced into the orb surrounding the shard, its seat fabric caught fire with a bright blue flame. The chair's trajectory remained unchanged, though, and it connected with the artifact, knocking it loose from its position. Rob heard the chair, and likely the shard, clatter to the platform as the orb sputtered and partially collapsed. The eastern half of the platform machinery continued to electrify the pedestal and in turn the pedestal continued to focus the energy into an orb, but it looked much less robust as it fed the rift.

Tillinghast snapped around after the chair smashed into the

platform he was standing on, cutting off his chanting mid-syllable. "You again!" he shouted at Rob. He lowered his arms and the tendrils from the rift just wiggled their way up his arms, across his shoulders, and to the top of his head, the point of his body now nearest the edge of the tear. An aura of orange and green undulated around him like a shaken lava lamp.

The rift shivered again and its rate of growth dropped dramatically. Without Tillinghast feeding it, the rift expansion had slowed to a crawl. He could still see chunks of the ceiling and back wall flaking off and drifting away into the space on the other side. But stopping Tillinghast more permanently still seemed to be the best bet.

Two ladders led to the platform and Rob lurched up the closest on the right side, trying to use this momentary distraction to close the gap on Tillinghast. He should have brought a gun. He really hadn't been considering that he might need some equipment to assist with killing a genocidal psychotic. It would have to be a good old brawl.

Tillinghast turned and reached out toward Rob. Rob broke into a run to try to cover the last dozen feet between them, but faltered slightly, seeing Tillinghast's eyes. They were no longer human. Where they should have been were now two small clusters of tiny eyes, matching the colors of the points of light in the ever-widening rift above them.

With a tinny echo, what was once Tillinghast uttered, "Bullets and electricity have no sway with you, it seems. How about we just vaporize you instead?"

A bright blue wall of fire shot from Tillinghast's outstretched arms and chewed through Rob's skin, stopping him in his tracks. He turned to his side, bracing himself as if against a gale-force wind. He felt his skin evaporating just as he lost his sight. Without his vision, he could only sense where his body was and feel the intermittent sting of heat as he regenerated and then had his nerves burned away again. He couldn't recruit any additional muscle power to forward motion.

With the one ear out of the rush of cosmic fire, Rob heard Tillinghast say, "Oh, well, quite a draw we have. I'm patient. You're not getting any stronger ... but I am."

Rob could feel the fires creeping deeper through his body. He went down to one leg as he felt his body repairing itself, but not quite as fast as Tillinghast could cook it away. As the side of his skull started to flake away, he quickly couldn't think as clearly.

Rift

Immobile and displaced, Hani was relieved to see the dome of tentacles had stopped growing. She waited, hoping she would start drifting to safety soon. Hanging out in the smoking remains of the reactor chamber really wasn't going to be much help. Several more seconds went by before she sensed that something was different. It took her a few more seconds before she realized the sky wasn't rotating. She wasn't in fast-forward at all, she was just stopped.

She tried to shove herself toward the remains of the reactor chamber blast doors, but she couldn't find a way to get a grip on her momentum. Her internal clock ticked away but the world stayed frozen. Had Rob failed? If she was too close to the rift to survive and the rift was never going to collapse, where was the safest place to be? How could she outrun it? She had no directional control and time was stuck. This felt like a pointless exercise.

As suddenly as it had stopped, the sky dislodged and started moving. At the same time, Hani's perspective got yanked through the blast doors and she was thrown back into the reactor access corridor. Something flashed from the door down the hall, past her, and out of sight behind her. The blast doors receded faster than she'd ever experienced her drifting before and in a moment she found herself standing at the intersection of the reactor access corridors and Amplification Chamber ramp. Time was running in full color again.

Hani bent over and vomited. The hallway spun. A blur of

control room windows and the ramp twisted past her vision and she slammed onto her side. She lay motionless, trying to gain control of her body. As the dizziness started to fade, her eyes focused down the western reactor hallway. Someone was running away from her toward the blast doors. She was pretty sure she had the same T-shirt. And jeans.

Hani pushed herself upright and snapped her head to the left, looking down the ramp. Rob was pressing a button on a control panel. The roll-up door slid up several feet and he ducked under it, moving out of sight. She tried to call out, but her throat refused to behave. She coughed instead, clearing the last of the vomit from her mouth. She shuffled to all fours and looked down the corridor again. The figure had reached the blast doors and took a few steps backward before breaking into a run and suddenly vanishing with a distant popping noise, barely audible over the crackling and droning coming through the now halfway open roll-up door. Could the nearest place of safety found for her by her abilities have been the past?

Hani spat a few more times and wiped her mouth. The top of her hand came back bloody. Checking her nose, she smeared more blood from her discovered nose bleed. She wondered if she was finally dying. She brought up one knee and lifted herself to her feet slowly. Her vestibular system hadn't entirely recovered.

She stood for a moment, swaying, and heard gun fire from the Amplification Chamber. That was unlikely to stop Rob. She turned away from the reactor that she was going to have destroyed and started a shuffling jog toward the final reactor chamber. In what seemed like minutes, she finally got to the end of the hall, bracing a blood-covered hand on the blast door. She panted for a few breaths. Hani stood up fully and raised her arms out away from her body like she was going to start making a snow angel.

In her earlier efforts, Hani had always used a sense of momentum as a hint for triggering the displacement of her position. This time, she reached out, feeling where she needed to be instead of where she was, and just willed herself through the steel. There was a momentary flash of gray and the second reactor column manifested itself in full color to her. She stood, arms still outstretched, four feet beyond the blast doors. A headache like a pair of giant steel-tipped wedges blasted its way into her temples and she clutched at her head, screaming.

When Hani came to, her face was stuck to the floor in a small pool of blood. She reminded herself to try avoiding fast displacements for the rest of her possibly short life. She sat up and the room spun a few times before settling down.

"Well, no barfing at least," Hani observed to herself. She checked her watch, trying to figure out how long she'd been out. Realizing the futility of expecting her watch to have any better a sense of how time was passing, she dropped her wrist and stood back up. The room was configured identically to the first. She stood up and stumbled toward the fire ax. The world flickered gray and she swore.

Ignoring the unlikely-to-be-hazardous contents of the coolant, Hani rounded the humming plasma silo and started cracking away at the nearest blue pipe. With her newly honed pipe-splitting skills, coolant burst from the pipe in two hits. The world flashed gray from another radiation surge. They were too close together. She's lost too much time lying on the floor.

She hit the next pipe twice and it split, pouring pressurized coolant across her legs and onto the floor. It was much warmer than she'd expected, but not unmanageable. It felt like she'd been pushed into a hot tub on high, not like getting a pot of boiling water dumped on her.

She focused on not losing track of her swings against the third pipe as the world kept flickering into gray as the surges stacked up again. She landed the pipe-splitting hit just as the world flipped gray and the coolant drained out in fast-forward. One pipe remained intact. She wondered if the reactor could still run on a quarter of its cooling capacity. She counted out the seconds, but noticed she was already drifting to the right, roughly in the direction of the Amplification Chamber.

At count 6, she'd passed through the swirling plasma in the reactor. At count 8, the silo's containment failed, consuming the chamber in a cloud of concrete and rebar. By count 10 she was surrounded by dirt and clay slipping past her perspective. At count 20, a new room appeared. It clicked into full color and she dropped to the floor, tasting blood again.

She was in a room filled with racks of computer equipment. Between machines she could catch glimpses of the Amplification Chamber, the vastness of the tear, and some kind of high energy blue light show taking place on a raised platform. She ran down the aisle of racks and rounded a corner, shoving chairs out of the way. In the corner of the room were a pair of bloodied handcuffs and an expended Taser. The conduction wires lay splayed in a loose pile.

She turned and ran through a bent wire mesh door. As she ran to the left behind an aisle of control consoles in the main chamber, she tried to understand what she was seeing ahead of her. On the walls to either side of the platform were giant bulging cracks from floor to ceiling. To the back of the room and mostly above her was the pin-pricked luminous void of the rift. At the front of the platform was some kind of pedestal. Next to that was a man who appeared to be pouring blue flames from his arms. Tendrils of light attached his head to the edges of the rift.

Passing a prone body dressed as a guard, Hani came left around to the eastern side of the platform. The ceiling was crumbling as the rift was slowly shrinking. Small chunks of concrete and plaster rained into the chamber. She carefully climbed up the eastern ladder to the platform, trying to stay low. Beyond the man who must have been Tillinghast, she saw the focus of the blue flames. A burning skeleton was crouched on its knees, with arms crossed in front of its averted skull. At the center of skeleton's ribcage was a throbbing red sphere, with protruding glowing white spikes. It spun slowly, seemingly unbattered by the roaring flames directed its way. This had to be what was left of Rob.

Chips of Rob's bone and meat tore away, flung clear of the platform, only to be rapidly replaced by fresh pieces, but Tillinghast seemed to be gaining ground. One blackened skeletal arm crumbled and went careening off the edge of the platform.

Hani surveyed the rest of the platform. At the back was a smoking overturned office chair. Between the chair and Tillinghast lay her shard. She smiled despite herself. She hadn't seen it in almost 70 years but she recognized it immediately. Above it, in the void, the stars had started collecting near the edge of the rift closest to the shard. She stared at the eyes and heard voices. They wanted to help her. Help her collect the artifact.

Rob's jaw dislodged and caught briefly on his spine before spinning away. Hani snapped out of her trance and tried to figure out how to stop Tillinghast. He looked to be entirely absorbed on his eradication of Rob. He was surrounded with a wavering orange aura that seemed to be turning the platform red-hot under his shoes. His shoes were impossibly unburned, along with the rest of him. Sticking out from his waistband, Hani saw a pistol.

Hani approached, not needing to be quiet in the din of the crackling torrent of flames. She reached for the gun and the world snapped to gray the moment she was going to have made contact with Tillinghast's surrounding aura. She mentally shoved, displacing herself back a few inches, and returned to the world. In her absence Rob had been further reduced, with both arms, one leg, and his skull now missing.

Hani turned and crossed the platform to the office chair, hefting it overhead. She sneaked back behind Tillinghast and swung the chair at the small of his back. It was not subtle. The chair made contact and started to smoke, melting plastic and burning paint off the metal. The wheels caught the gun and pitched it under the pedestal. Hani carried her swing through, tossing the chair into the consoles below.

Tillinghast howled and pinched out the rush of flames, turning to find his new assailant. He faced Hani. The two clusters of tiny eyes roiled against his squinting lids. His mouth hung open, bellowing with rage. Bristling between his lips and gums, bundles of thin tentacles twisted, searching for purchase on his face.

Hani bent and retrieved the gun. Behind Tillinghast, she watched as the glowing red ball of white spikes wrapped itself in organs. She stood, raising the pistol to what served as Tillinghast's face. Tillinghast clenched his jaw and bared his teeth. He let loose a blast of fire, but Hani ceased to exist.

Rob's muscles poured around his organs and bones, filling in gaps and tightening his body into a human shape.

Presuming successful vaporization of Hani, Tillinghast dropped the wall of flame, only to have her snap instantly into existence. She shot him point-blank between the eyes and his head snapped back.

The orange aura sputtered out and he dropped to the platform like a pile of bricks.

Rob stood slowly, steadying himself on the platform railing. The void's tendrils of light edged away from Tillinghast, waving in the air slowly like snakes finding their next meal.

"You okay, Rob?" Hani asked, holding the pistol tightly, still staring at Tillinghast's corpse.

"That was ... disorienting. It was like being asleep. Only much less relaxing," Rob said, releasing the railing. "You got the reactors down?" He nodded at the bulging walls.

"Yeah."

"Are *you* okay?" Rob said, pointing at the blood caked on Hani's shirt and face.

"I may have pushed my limits a bit," Hani said.

"Yeah, I can—" Rob was cut short by Tillinghast's head lolling over and splitting in half. A creature covered in bulbous tentacles dragged itself from the exit wound in Tillinghast's skull, cracking the opening wider as it emerged. The clusters of eyes inflated slightly, now looking like tight bunches of grapes covered in slime. The tendrils from the rift edge started maneuvering toward the abomination.

"Shit, shit, shit!" Hani lowered the pistol and emptied the magazine at it. It sprayed a gray fluid with each bullet impact, but the holes filled in and it grew slightly with each shot. She kicked it and it skittered off the platform, making a wet noise as it landed on the floor beneath them. Small tentacles sprouted from toe of her boot.

"Get that boot off!" Rob shouted, crouching over Tillinghast's body. Rob grabbed Tillinghast's lab coat and yanked it up over Tillinghast's arms and the remains of his head.

Hani was one step ahead, tearing at her boot laces. She kicked the boot off and peeled her sock off, inspecting her foot. No sign of corruption.

Rob wrapped the lab coat around the boot and tossed it up into the void. The searching tendrils tracked the motion. The boot wavered as it crossed the event horizon and started drifting away into the void with the stars watching it. The lab coat fluttered back to the platform.

"We gotta catch that thing," Hani blurted, grabbing the coat and scampering to the closest ladder.

Rob shimmied down the other, now flame-blackened, ladder and rounded the base of the platform. Hani came around the other side, carefully avoiding a gray slime trail the creature had left in its undulatory wake. It was closing in on the fallen guard's body.

Hani leapt forward, tackling the writhing blob in the lab coat. It hissed and burbled as she stood and retreated back around to the ladder, climbing with one hand, holding the coat out behind her. A few tentacles had bored through the coat as she climbed. Rob followed her up the ladder.

The mass in the collected lab coat had gotten heavier. "I'm not going to be able to get this thing to the rift," Hani admitted, hauling it up over the edge of the platform with both arms now.

"Here, pass it up to me," Rob said, climbing up precariously on the pedestal.

Hani dragged the improvised sack and lifted it up, keeping her face from the wiggling appendages that had emerged. She transferred her grip on the coat to Rob.

Rob spun in place on the pedestal, doing his best naked Greek Olympian discus throw impression, gathering momentum. He twisted the trajectory and spun the coat bundle up into the rift. He lost his balance and tumbled backward off the platform as the bagged creature squirmed through the air. Like the lost boot, the collection of fabric and tentacles shimmered briefly and then floated up into the void, no longer influenced by gravity.

Hani ran to the railing to check on Rob. "You alright?"

"Yeah," Rob replied, "I just broke my neck. Briefly. No big deal."

Hani laughed and sagged against the railing, trying to catch her breath.

Rob was rolling the guard out of his jacket. Serving as a one-sided loin cloth, he tied the jacket's arms across his waist at the back, saying, "It's a bit breezy in here."

He looked up at the panting, blood-covered Hani. "Could you do me a favor? I think you're the only one with a boot. Pulverize that shard, would you?" He came around the platform and pulled himself back up the ladder.

Hani turned and looked up at the crackling tear in space. The tendrils had shrunk considerably, along with the rift itself. They looked lost, feeling the air for somewhere to touch. She hitched over to her shard and paused, studying the writing. The voices came into focus again as she approached. She bent over, reaching for it.

"Boot!" Rob cried out. "Hani, don't pick it up!" He stayed near the edge of the platform. The tendrils had started reaching out toward him.

Hani blinked and lifted her head to look at the endless sea of eyes watching her from the rift. She straightened up again and raised her arm to the void, middle finger extended. She brought up her heel and slammed it down on the shard, crushing it.

There was an audible rumble as the tendrils got sucked back into the rift. The once-spherical void started to collapse back to a vertical, pointy, egg-shaped tear. Concrete, clay, and sand from the surface continued to filter down into the chamber around the perimeter of what prevailed of the edges of the ceiling.

Rob crossed the platform to stand next to Hani. She was grinding the last of the ceramic into dust under her boot. He hugged her and she returned the embrace. The rift shrank and crackled into nothingness. They looked up, watching proper stars shining back at them from the open Nevada sky.